THE
GRAVE
ABOVE THE
GRAVE

THE
GRAVE
ABOVE THE
GRAVE

Bernard Kerik

Humanix Books

The Grave Above the Grave

Copyright © 2018 by Humanix Books
All rights reserved.
Humanix Books, P.O. Box 20989, West Palm Beach, FL 33416, USA
www.humanixbooks.com | info@humanixbooks.com

Library of Congress Cataloging-in-Publication Data is available upon request.

Humanix Books is a division of Humanix Publishing, LLC. Its trademark, consisting of the word "Humanix," is registered in the Patent and Trademark Office and in other countries.

ISBN: 978-1-63006-099-2 (Hardcover)
ISBN: 978-1-63006-100-5 (E-book)

Printed in the United States of America
10 9 8 7 6 5 4 3 2 1

For Maverick Michael and Benjamin Matthew,
and my mother, Clara Kerik

....

ACKNOWLEDGMENTS

This book was made possible with the help and support of many, but first and foremost, my thanks goes to my good friend Christopher Ruddy, who came up with the idea and encouraged me to give it a shot. I also want to thank Mary Glenn and her team at Humanix Publishing for all their help and support; to Marc Eliot, a legendary writer and storyteller who constantly challenged me for more, and then had to clean up my scribble and grammatical errors once I gave it to him; and to Ken Chandler, for his editorial review and insights. To friends old and new, like Anthony Ambrose, Nathan Berman, Matt Bissonette, Simon Cohen, Daniel Del Valle, Howard Jonas, Shmuel Jones, Elie Katz, JM, Albert Manzo, and Sly Stallone—thank you for your friendship, support, and inspiration when I needed it most; and to my friends and former colleagues that have served, or still serve, in the military and in local, state, and federal law enforcement—thank you for your support, insight, ideas, and stories, and more so, your sacrifice and heroism . . . this country owes you a debt of gratitude that it can never justly repay. Last and most importantly, to Angelina, Celine, Jacqui, Joe, and Hala—thank you for your love, support, and inspiration during this project, even during some extremely difficult and trying times. I can only pray that better is yet to come.

Certainly there is no hunting like the hunting of man
and those who have hunted armed men long enough and liked it,
never really care for anything else thereafter.

ERNEST HEMINGWAY, "ON THE BLUE WATER," *ESQUIRE*, APRIL 1936

CHAPTER 1

1:10 am, Wednesday, 4 October

For the third time in a week, the phone began screaming at just after one in the morning, sounding, in the bedroom, as loud as a three-alarmer. In the drawn-shade dark, Sheilah, who was sleeping on the side of the bed nearest to the landline's nightstand, reached over, lifted the cordless receiver, and wordlessly, in one unbroken swoop, passed it over her otherwise sleeping body to the instantly awake Rick Raymond.

Without looking directly at her, he took the phone from her hand and placed it to his ear. The caller was Jerry Gallagher, his chief of staff, sounding, as always, calm, intense, urgent, and methodical. "Commissioner . . . two cops shot, one DOA, one likely." Cop speak for one dead, one probably going to die. Raymond automatically cranked up the police band radio he kept on the night table closest to him, and the crackling voice confirmed the shooting. He knew original field input was wrong 95 percent of the time, but when Jerry said it, it was good as gold.

"Where," Raymond said evenly. Then, without waiting for an answer, he added, "Has the mayor been notified?"

"Times Square, 44th and Broadway. The mayor's detail has been notified." His tone became more intimate. "Some fuckin' lunatic walked right up to the police car and opened fire."

"Christ." Raymond took a hard breath. "See you at Bellevue." He reached back over Sheilah, who was now wide-eyed and looking at him, and dropped the receiver back into its cradle. Then he stumbled over to the bathroom, took a shot of bitter green mouthwash, spit it into the sink when it started to sting, splashed cold water on his face, leaned in quickly to check his hair, brushed his thick bush back, rubbed his fingers across his stubbled chin, good enough for this hour, reached for the drip-dry suit hanging behind the door, slid into it quickly, like it was a one-zip circus costume, pulled on his black socks, and slipped into his laced shoes and headed out.

"Do I need to get up?" Sheilah said, from bed, sounding as if she had cotton in her mouth and was talking in her sleep.

"Not now, but you're going to have a busy day. I've got two cops shot in Times Square; your office is probably on the way."

He came over and kissed her warm face, then quietly slipped out the door and walked down the hall to the building's elevator bank. He rode down the seven flights to the lobby of his Riverdale apartment, where he was met by Jonathan Archer, his bodyguard—"Eagle One." Archer, a highly decorated African-American detective, who happened to look more like a model for *GQ* than an officer of the NYPD, was the head of Raymond's security posse. Because of the way Archer and his team presented themselves, Sammy Breshill, writing in the *New York Herald*, had dubbed them "Raymond's Fashion Force." Now, as always, Archer never showed any visible sign of fatigue, even though 30 minutes earlier he had been fast asleep on a cot in the Five-0, the nearby precinct that covered the commissioner's residence.

As Raymond approached, Archer began to speak in his familiar force-field staccato: "Both families were taken to Bellevue. One is from Nassau; one is from Westchester. Both cops were on the job for about two years—same academy class; the DOA was married just four months ago; the other not married. The suspect, Hispanic or light-skinned black male, ran from the scene and we believe got on a northbound A Train at 43rd and Broadway; he hasn't been seen since."

Outside, in front of Raymond's apartment building, the commissioner's black Suburban sat gleaming in the streetlights, the SUV's colored emergency lights rotating, the vehicle looking like a four-wheel Chevy spaceship from Mars. Two marked NYPD highway unit cars were also there, one in front, one behind the commissioner's SUV. Raymond slid into the back seat of the Suburban and nodded to his personal driver, Taylor Shelby, "Eagle Two." Shelby was a longtime member of the "Fashion Force," having worked with Raymond since years before, when both were in narcotics. He had earned his place on Raymond's elite team, which meant he was on call 24/7. As soon as Archer got in the front seat, all three vehicles took off—sirens screaming and lights spinning, lighting up the Bronx like some dipsy midnight street fair. The three-car motorcade drove to the Henry Hudson Parkway southbound, en route to Manhattan's Bellevue Hospital. As they sped downtown, additional highway units fell in behind.

The phone in the SUV rang; Archer answered. It was "Eagle Three," Mike Tonaka, "Tokyo Mike" for short, Raymond's advance man. It was Tonaka's job to already be wherever the commissioner was headed, and to know everything there Raymond needed to know. He was calling from the hospital to inform Archer that New York City's mayor, Joseph Brown, was 15 minutes away from arrival. Archer relayed the information over his shoulder to the commissioner. Raymond leaned forward and told Shelby to step on it. He wanted to be there before Brown. The phone rang again. Archer picked up, listened, and then asked into the phone, "Do they have the shooter?"

"Negative," a duty captain from headquarters operations said. "Apparently, he disappeared into the subway; we have a few witnesses telling us that he may have jumped on a northbound A Train, but that's all we have." Archer repeated the information to Raymond.

Fuck, the commissioner thought to himself. There are so many live cameras in Times Square, with lenses so tight and sharp they can read the time off a perp's watch. They'll figure it out as soon as they examine the footage in the cameras.

Archer repeated the question to the captain, "Do they have the shooter?," listened, and then said back to Raymond, "Suspect ran into the subway entrance on 43rd and Broadway." Raymond blew an angry breath of air through his puffed cheeks as he shook his head back and forth. He looked at his watch: 2:30. It was going to be an even longer night now.

The 'cade turned left onto 34th Street, joined by two more police vehicles, and they all sped east like an iron and steel parade across the island to Bellevue's emergency room entrance at the east end of 34th, just before it bleeds into the East River Drive. When they arrived, dozens of cops had already gathered in front of and around the hospital's emergency room section. Everybody and his fuckin' brother, Raymond thought to himself, and of course a shitload circus of pool reporters that the highway cops had corralled behind hastily erected barricades about 25 feet from the emergency room door. As he exited the Suburban, they thrust their microphones and cameras in his direction. He brushed past them, escorted by a number of uniformed officers, and said nothing as he pushed through the double doors and entered the emergency room area, where an entire section had been cordoned off, entry allowed only for medical personnel, police, and immediate family.

He could feel his fingers of both hands tighten into balls as he approached the first set of curtains and heard a woman wailing at the top of her lungs. As the cops pulled back the curtain, he saw the dead cop's bereft parents and new bride standing in a small circle as they were being consoled by a Catholic priest and an NYPD chaplain. The mother was bent over, weeping into a handkerchief, her husband's left arm around her, holding her up. The bride's intermittent screams echoed down the hall, as if she were being continually stabbed. Raymond went over to them and hugged the mother. It was his rule to always go to the mother first. He whispered in her ear and assured her the entire force was there for her, and gave her his solemn word that her son's killer would be caught. He then moved to the bride, who was now rocking back and forth, her mouth open, her screams now a garbled choke, her face tracked with tears, her thick and curly brown hair shocked into a disheveled web. He put his hands on her shoulders. "You have to be strong for them," he said, nodding to the dead cop's parents. That was like pulling the plug on the ocean. She burst into loud, groaning sobs and buried her face in his chest; her body began jerking uncontrollably. He held her for as long as he could, until he heard a commotion in the hallway, and passed her off to the professionally calm chaplain.

Before he could get there, the hallway's wide double doors slammed against the wall as they were pushed open by an entourage of suits, followed by Mayor Joseph Brown. He strode in, jaw first, his Florsheim shoes clacking loudly against the hard hospital floor. His black suit shone nearly white under the hospital's neon lighting. His comb-over was in disarray as a result of Brown's nervous habit of running his fingers along his scalp during a time of crisis, the carefully set strands pushed nearly all the way back now, revealing just how little hair he really had. He was surrounded by a small army of his security team and hospital personnel.

Raymond went directly to the mayor, who continued his stride as they shook hands, hard and quick, then huddled for a few minutes, pit-of-the-stomach stuff, after which Raymond led him over to the family of the dead cop. Brown tried his best, and failed, to look warm.

Raymond then took the mayor behind another curtain so they could meet the family of the surviving 24-year-old officer who was in surgery. He had taken a bullet to his left shoulder, and one in the face that had passed from the right side of his jaw to the left. The mayor offered his best wishes and prayers to the family and assured them that the city was going to do everything possible to get the shooter.

After, the mayor and Raymond reconnoitered with the chief of department, Joe Allegra; the first deputy commissioner, Joe Nagle, technically the number two in command of the department; and the deputy commissioner of public information, Tom Thomas, whose job it was to be Raymond's eyes and ears with the media—to make sure Raymond knew what they knew, what they would ask, and what they would be looking for, and to make sure there were no surprises coming when Raymond and the mayor met the press. The four reviewed everything that had happened so far that night—what they had, which wasn't much; what they wanted, which was a lot; and what they were going to do next. Raymond said it was incredible to him that the shooter had managed to slip down the rabbit hole of a New York City subway station in the midst of the panic that he had created, somehow managing to avoid running into any on-duty or even off-duty cops. "He's either very lucky or very smart," he said, and then told his chief of staff, Jerry Gallagher, to make sure they were reviewing all security footage immediately pulled from every northbound station on the entire Eighth Avenue line, north and southbound. "I want every frame of that video examined under a fuckin' microscope until I know what this guy ate yesterday."

"One last thing," Chief of Department Allegra said to Raymond. "According to a half-dozen eyewitnesses close enough to the car when the shooter opened fire, they all say they heard him scream, "*Allahu Akbar!* God is great!'"

Raymond felt the back of his neck ice up. His lips folded into themselves. An act of terror was the last thing he wanted this to be. In the 16 years after 9/11, the day the NYPD lost 23 good cops and he lost his wife, he had risen through the ranks of the NYPD and continually swore that this would never again happen on his watch, not to his officers and not to the citizens of New York City they were sworn to protect. He had been able to keep that vow, until now. He immediately told Allegra to increase the public threat level and to enhance security on all the city's soft targets—churches, synagogues, and any other potential religious targets.

Outside the door of the emergency room, the press pool had grown to about 20 reporters, who were becoming increasingly impatient for an update, something that could make the morning headlines or lead a live break-in on TV. Raymond and the mayor walked out the ER door, and the instantaneous flashes of so many cameras created a momentary strobe effect on the rear entrance of the building.

Together they walked to the bank of microphones that had been set up, and waited for the buzzing and the photos to stop. As per protocol, the mayor spoke first. He cleared his throat, nervously ran a hand over his scalp, adjusted his glasses with the other, and began: "This is a very sad day for our people, and the men and women of the New York City Police Department." He thanked the hospital staff for their fine work, reassured the public everything was under control, and reminded them that if they saw anything that would be of help they should immediately call the police. He ended his comments with a moment of silent prayer, then turned the microphones over to Raymond, who read from his own hurriedly scribbled notes as he summarized what had taken place: ". . . deceased . . . critical, likely to live . . . Times Square . . . subway . . . got away . . ." He then politely but firmly fielded a rush of questions for which he had no answers, and ended by promising to get the latest developments to them as soon as he had anything new.

As the press pool began to break down, with Raymond still at the microphone bank, the reporter Sammy Breshill darted up to him, stuck a small digital recorder in his face, and asked, "Is it true, Commissioner, that the perp was yelling '*Allahu Akbar*' as he shot into the car?"

Raymond wanted to punch him, for this and for a lot of things Breshill had written about Raymond through the years. Instead, keeping his balled fists by his side, he brushed past him. Raymond's rule for talking to the press never varied: Don't answer a question that you don't want to answer, because it will inevitably lead to another question that you don't want to answer, and then you can't stop, deny, or control the outflow of information. By saying nothing you don't confirm any part of a story, and likely nothing will run. He was joined by Archer, who turned and said to Breshill, "The press conference is over. Don't sandbag the commissioner, Breshill."

"Just doing my job, Jon," Breshill said. "Yours is to protect Raymond. Mine is to get the story and inform the public of it."

"You're a dick," Archer said.

He and Raymond then walked through the emergency room parking lot to where the Suburban was idling, its front and back passenger doors already opened by Shelby. Raymond slid in the back, and Archer slammed the door, then got in the front. Shelby gunned it, swirling around a dozen other marked and unmarked police cars and out onto the street.

Breshill watched the SUV leave from the bottom of the exit. His nose told him there was more of a story here than Raymond was letting on, and he was going to get it. First.

In the silence, Raymond suddenly cursed out loud, meant for neither Shelby nor Archer. *"Motherfucker!"* Then he took a deep breath, threw his head back, and squeezed his eyes with the thumb and index finger of his right hand. "How the hell did Breshill find that out?" he asked Archer.

"That prick knows everything. Ever since he's become the star of the *New York Herald*, he's become the self-appointed guardian-of-the-people."

There was silence until they got to Park Avenue, when Raymond said to Archer, "I want to see where those kids were shot." Archer repeated the command to Shelby, then raised his arm to his mouth and talked into the small black microphone that peeked out from his sleeve. "Eagle One to Eagle Three. The commissioner is not heading to his residence. I repeat—the commissioner is not heading to his residence. We're heading over to 44 and Broadway. We're 15 out."

Raymond wanted to call Sheilah and leave her a message for when she got up, to tell her that he was all right but not sure when he would be back, but before they crossed Madison, he had leaned his head back, hoping to catch a few quick ZZZs.

I had always wanted to be a police officer, to protect the city I loved. Just out of high school, barely 18 years old, I spent three years in the U.S. Army, training that proved invaluable for me when I was honorably discharged. I enrolled in John Jay University, to study criminal justice. At 25, I received my BS degree, and joined the New York City Police Department. I came up through the ranks, and in 1999 became a captain, and the following year, took command of the 1st Precinct in Lower Manhattan. I was determined to keep the city safe and great. I had no idea then, how difficult and horrendous that pledge would turn out to be.

I remember rushing toward the Towers on September 11, 2001. I was 37 years old. I was working in the 1st Precinct when the calls came in. Two planes had hit the Twin Towers, throw-ing the city into chaos and the world into monstrous disorder. The affected areas of Lower Manhattan, south of Houston Street, were originally divided into seven zones, Zone 1 more commonly referred to as Ground Zero. That's where I headed. I wasn't sure, no one was, how bad the damage was, how many officers we had lost or were wounded, if the city was going to be standing when the sun went down. I gritted my teeth, deter-mined to do whatever I could, for anybody who needed my help, even as my official car sped directly into Hell. I wanted to save my friends, my compadres, my family. Who did they think they were that they could hit the greatest city in the world. Just when I thought it couldn't get any worse, I heard the news; in addition to the attack in New York City, the Pentagon had been hit, and a flight had gone down in Shanksville, Pennsylvania. United Flight 93. My heart stopped. I couldn't breathe. My wife, Mary, was on that flight out of Newark to San Francisco. I wanted to make them pay . . . I still do . . .

Here we go again, Raymond thought to himself, as his memories slowly morphed into a dream and he fitfully slipped into a brief but deep sleep.

CHAPTER 2

3:55 am, Wednesday, 4 October

Raymond snapped awake just as the Suburban pulled up to 44th and Broadway, having been passed through the police line. Times Square and its immediate perimeter, from 41st to 46th, Seventh Avenue and Broadway, had been completely shut down and sealed off. He and Archer got out and walked down to the immediate crime scene. "My God," Raymond thought, as they got closer to the bullet-blistered police vehicle. "It looks like Sonny's car on the Causeway." He then turned and said to a two-star chief, the uniformed Manhattan Borough commander, "Anything from the cameras yet?"

"Affirmative," the commander said. "We definitely got him getting on a northbound A Train, but don't know where he got off." Raymond thanked him, and he and Archer proceeded to walk the area, still buzzing with dozens of uniforms making notes, taking photos, talking on phones, and keeping civilians and the press behind the yellow lines. Many of them had never met the commissioner, or even seen him in person before, except the day they were sworn in, and Raymond made it a point to stop and talk to every one of them, shake their hands, and offer a few words of thanks, reminding them all to be careful.

He and Archer then returned to the Suburban and got in. "Let's go home," Raymond said. Archer spoke into the mike on his sleeve. "Eagle One to Eagle Three. We're heading for the Castle." Shelby navigated west via 45th Street. When he reached the West Side Highway, he made a right and slipped into the flow of traffic headed north. As he did so, he killed the flashers. It was 6:35 am. There was little outbound traffic and not yet a heavy flow on the other side, coming into the city. To the left, the Hudson River looked shining and inviting, like a high-priced call girl.

The peace was interrupted by the beeping of the police radio. The dispatcher's crackling voice came on and said, "A confirmed 10-13 over division in the Two-Six, vicinity of 125th Street and Broadway." That got Raymond's attention—a 10-13, officer needs assistance in the 26th Precinct. The dispatcher continued, "Two-Six anticrime is in pursuit of a suspect fitting the description of the suspect in the Midtown South shooting." Now Raymond bolted up and forward. Archer switched the radio to the Two-Six's frequency, the precinct that covered 125th Street. "Shots fired Central! Two-Six sergeant to Central. Shots fired . . . cop down at one-two-five and Broadway . . . get a bus . . . suspect running toward the Westside Highway just off Broadway!"

Raymond hugged the back of the front seat as Shelby floored the Suburban, turned on the siren, and flipped the flashers back on. He took the exit at 125th Street hard, then slammed on the brakes as he skidded into a curve, exiting the highway onto the ramp, making a right on 125th toward Broadway. They could hear other police vehicles heading in the same direction, and their sirens got louder as Raymond's Suburban got closer. Midway between Broadway and the Westside Highway, they saw about eight uniformed and plain-clothes cops running after a man, *who was heading straight toward the Suburban.* "*That's the guy!*" Raymond yelled, pointing at the run-ner. In pursuit, an unmarked car, with siren blaring, blew through a stop sign. The suspect bolted to his left, pivoted, and fired a pistol at the oncoming car. "*Hit that motherfucker!*" Raymond screamed at Shelby, and he, Shelby, and Archer braced themselves as they slammed head-on into the other vehicle, the suspect caught between the two. He shrieked once, crazily, as blood spurted from his eyes, his nose, his mouth, his ears, and then he went silent, as blood, like a red geyser, spurted up from a hole in the top of his head.

Raymond managed to kick open his accordioned door and get out. Shelby and Archer had been saved by their airbags, and they, too, were able to exit the vehicle. The three then rushed to where two officers struggled to jerk the dead body loose from between the two cars. The driver behind the unmarked vehicle was finally able to start it and put it into reverse. The engine rattled loudly as he rolled the car back slowly, just enough to have the suspect drop, his lower extrem-ities covered in blood, piss, and shit. Several uniformed officers had by now arrived and began setting up a perimeter, as Raymond began to search for the perp's gun. One of the officers checked for a pulse, confirming the obvious.

All of a sudden, every uniformed and plainclothes cop there, perhaps 20 of them at this point, just stood there staring at Raymond. No one moved. Then one heavy-set sergeant in uniform broke the ice and said softly, "Holy fuck, the PC killed the cop killer . . ." The other cops didn't know if they should cheer, laugh, or remain stoic, while the police radios went ballistic that Car 1, the police commis-sioner's car, was involved in the pursuit and hit the perp.

Raymond could feel the nausea cooking up in his stomach. He stood up, so far unable to find the perp's gun, and pulled out his cell to call the mayor, when the phone started ringing in his hand. He looked at it for a moment, saw it was the mayor, and hit the answer button. Always first, Raymond flashed to himself. "Is it true?" he heard the mayor ask. "You killed the suspect?" Before Raymond could say anything, the mayor added, "With your fucking *car? Are you okay?*" The mayor went on, "Meet me in City Hall at 8 am. Did you notify Dannis yet?"

Raymond was sure now he was going to throw up. "No sir, but I will. See you then."

What the mayor didn't know when he asked that question was that the saber-sharp Manhattan DA Sheilah Dannis, a widow whose husband had died suddenly from cancer eight years earlier, was actually lying in his bed in his apartment in the Bronx. At the relatively young age of 44, she had become one of the most prominent prosecutors in the country, having moved steadily up the ladder, starting as a loyal first assistant to the former district attorney, who had held the office for 25 years until his overdue retirement. She had then run for the office herself. To her delight, and to the surprise of many—after all, this was still politically a testosterone-driven town—she was elected in a landslide. It also put the mayor's office in her career binoculars.

Dannis immediately became something of a media favorite due in no small part to the fact that she was photogenic. Cameras loved her dirty-blond good looks, her wide smile, and her friendly but no-nonsense manner. She was tall and slim and in great physical shape, all of which made her look at least a decade younger than her 44 years. Every morning, by 6:30, she was in the gym, working out, before going to her office, causing the tabloids to dub her "Wonder DA." The public loved it—and her.

That morning, just past six, the snooze alarm on her iPhone had done its thing, and she was gingerly getting out of bed. She had barely slept, the night filled with what seemed like nonstop phone calls from her office about the Times Square shooting. Little did her office staff know that she knew about the shooting long before they did, because she was lying next to the police commissioner when he was notified. She had hoped to get at least an uninterrupted hour or two of sleep before heading downtown, but it never happened. No stopping at the gym, either, not this morning. She took a quick shower and was about to head out, figuring to do her make-up in the car, when her cell phone began to ring again. She sighed. This was not going to stop. When she saw it was Raymond, she was happy it wasn't the office. "Hi," she said.

Before he could say anything, she got another call, this one from her chief of staff, Stephanie Mills, who was also her best friend; Mills had been with her from the beginning, when Dannis was working in the DA's office and Mills was assigned to narcotics. She told Raymond to hold, and clicked over. "What is it?"

"You haven't heard, have you. Rick killed the cop killer."

"*What?*"

As Mills began to fill in the details, Sheilah interrupted her to get back to Raymond on the other line. "He can fill me in," she said.

"Don't talk to him now," Mills snapped. "Have him call me. There's going to be a grand jury investigation, and we need to keep you out of it if we can. Disconnect, and I'll call Raymond. I'll just tell him why you can't talk."

Dannis said goodbye and shut her phone off, slipped on a light coat, and headed out the door.

CHAPTER 3

5:30 am, Wednesday, 4 October

Raymond wondered why Sheilah cut him off. He was about to re-speed dial, when his chief of staff, Jerry Gallagher, who had just arrived at the scene, came up to him. "Let me take a look at this bastard," Gallagher said. He asked a detective to show him the body, still on the ground, smelling like a mixture of fresh hot shit and vinegar piss, the blood pool starting to thicken into death jelly. He stood up, took a deep breath, and he and Raymond went over to his car, where Shelby and Archer were. Gallagher said he would take Raymond to City Hall, but Shelby and Archer were going to have to remain behind to do the accident report, and to meet with Internal Affairs to give a statement. Raymond would prepare his statement at the office later.

By now, dozens of NYPD uniforms from at least three precincts, along with members of the FBI JTTF—the Joint Terrorism Task Force—and other federal agents and the New York State Police, had gathered at the scene, as well as a group of reporters who were roped off about two blocks away. Detectives from the Two-Six continued to comb through the accident scene, interviewing the cops from the other car and bagging evidence. They put two cell phones they had found on the suspect's body into two separate bags, his wallet in another one, with his New Jersey driver's license taken out and placed face up. The name on it was Samir Abdullah Bakheer. It had a Main Street, Paterson, New Jersey, address.

JTTF ran the name and immediately discovered that Bakheer was already on their target list. They informed the Manhattan North duty inspector, Pat Kelly, that JTTF was handling the shooting of the two cops as a terror investigation. Also rolling up to the scene of the collision was Chelsea Jones, FBI assistant director of the New York field division. Jones was attractive, but focused on her job and not at all interested in winning official or after-hours beauty contests. She was tall, lean, and hard, with dark, straight hair parted on the side and pushed back, and wore a minimum amount of make-up. When she heard that the commissioner was involved, she was relieved. They were professional colleagues and personal friends, and had known each other for 16 years, all the way back to the dark days of 9/11.

Jones's driver was on his phone giving his office the suspect's address in Paterson and said, "Inspector, I just called the assistant U.S. attorney working this case to get a search warrant for the perp's house. Our guys are going to hit it in 30 minutes. If you want to get some people out to Paterson, they can join us and see what's what there."

Inspector Kelly immediately ordered one of his men, Sergeant Benning, to take a few police detectives out there, as two FBI agents jumped into their car. The detectives followed behind. The mini-caravan sped onto the Westside Highway up to the George

Washington Bridge and onto the upper level, and on the other side of the Hudson they picked up Interstate 80.

Following, not far behind, but not close enough to draw anyone's attention, Breshill drove his company's exhausted Honda Civic.

The FBI and the New York City cops arrived at the staging area and were greeted by about a dozen Paterson police. At the same time, 12 special FBI SWAT team members were preparing to hit the suspect's house. They had emerged from two black unmarked vans, armed with M4 machine guns. They were dressed completely in black, with black face masks and black helmets, with microphones and lights attached on top. Each wore a bulletproof vest, with a small embroidered American flag on the front, and the words "POLICE" in bold gray neon letters and "FBI," smaller, underneath, on the back. Their assignment was to enter the house and clear it of suspects, weapons, explosives. The local police, the NYPD, and the New York and New Jersey FBI agents watched in silence as the SWAT team split into two groups, the first moving to the front porch of the house, the other to the rear. The first group was about to hit the front door when two gunshots came from the rear of the house. No one moved or said a word, until the FBI's radio crackled: "Two shots fired. We have a dog down. Take the front door now."

Everyone exhaled.

The first group of agents boomed their way in and cleared to the rear of the house, where they met up with the rear group. Then the full team loaded into their vans and were gone, having never said a word to anyone. The on-site FBI supervisor, out of the Newark field division, came on the radio and announced to his people, "Okay, we've got a green light on entry."

NYPD Sergeant Benning and his detectives and the FBI agents entered the house along with three local uniforms. One room in the house appeared to have been used as an office. Underneath a bureau drawer in the bedroom, the FBI found three different passports in a plastic bag. Benning examined them. Each had a different name, and all had the suspect's face. The federal agents also found several boxes of 40mm cartridges, likely to match the ones used in the Midtown shooting, and a cache of assault weapons, dozens of ISIS black flags, and photocopies of *Inspire* strewn everywhere. In the back of a closet, an ISIS flag was draped across a wall. An agent pulled it down. It was covering an eight-inch hole, inside of which were a handgun and $20,000 in U.S. currency.

Benning and one of the FBI agents cataloged everything. Benning was sure this was the headquarters of the shooter, and that made it a federal jurisdiction case. Now he wanted to know why the shooter targeted the two cops in Times Square.

Among the small crowd that had gathered was Sammy Breshill, who had drawn the same conclusion as the cops and agents and wondered the same thing. Breshill knew this was going to be a national story, and would hit every newspaper and TV news show before noon. His goal was to find out the connection between the murders and Bakheer before anyone else and put that on the front page of the *New York Herald*.

With his byline.

CHAPTER 4

7:55 am, Wednesday, 4 October

Raymond sat in the passenger seat of the SUV as Gallagher drove to City Hall, while Archer, still back at the incident scene, filled them in over the speakerphone on the FBI raid in Paterson, as it came over the phone, and described what they'd found on Bakheer. The good news was that Raymond had personally taken Bakheer down. The bad news was that meant a mandatory grand jury. Under the present circumstances, that could problematic for both his professional and personal relationship with Dannis; the two had been seeing each other for close to three years, and had done everything in their power to keep it secret to avoid the press and possible conflicts of interest, him being New York City's top cop, and her being the district attorney responsible for prosecuting the NYPD's cases—and unfortunately prosecuting members of the NYPD when they went south.

To avoid the press, Raymond ordered the Intelligence Division, which controls City Hall security, to have all the reporters secured in the Blue Room until the mayor and he came in for the press briefing. Outside the mayor's office, a few reporters were standing around, sensing this was not the right time to approach Raymond and Gallagher as they got out of the SUV and walked up the stairs, into the building, escorted by four uniformed cops. Raymond's appearance, as the police commissioner, and as the city's and the country's latest folk hero, was national news, and that brought a press gathering not seen in years in the marble halls of City Hall. Many of the reporters inside and out had been there since dawn, as soon as the news of the Times Square shooting hit the wires. One newly assigned reporter to the City Hall police beat pelted Raymond with questions: "How does it feel to be a hero, Commissioner? Do we know yet who the shooter was?" Obviously, the FBI's raid had not hit yet, nor the identity of Bakheer. As Raymond hurried toward the mayor's office, one uniformed cop walked over to the reporter, mindful of the ever-present news cameras, gently but firmly blocking him from moving closer.

> *As the precinct commander of the 1st Precinct, I arrived at World Trade Center One within seven minutes after it was hit by the first plane. Standing on Vesey Street, I saw and heard people jumping all the way down from the 95th floor of that building, and I saw their bodies disintegrate into dust on impact. I'd been on the job 11 years by then, but had never seen anything like this before. I was stunned into a trance, as numbness took over my body to protect me from the unbelievable desperation of the jumpers and the depravity of the act that caused their desperation.*

Inside, the mayor was standing behind his desk, finishing up a phone call on his office landline. He hung up, walked around to shake Raymond's hand, gave him an obligatory hug, and asked him if he was okay. "Fine," Raymond said. The mayor coughed, poured himself a glass of water from a large pitcher on his desk, gestured for Raymond to sit down on one of the two big leather chairs that were tilted at an angle across from the desk, took a long drink, followed by a deep breath, then came around and unbuttoned his jacket as he sat in the other chair.

"So, give it."

Raymond told him everything he knew, and described in detail what had happened that morning, beginning with the phone call at two in the morning. The mayor listened intently, occasionally nodding his head up and down, slowly. Raymond thought he looked relieved, happy almost. Just then, the mayor's counsel, Michael Tierny, came in, his cloud of yellow hair leading the way. Raymond stood and shook his hand.

"The reason I'm here," Tierny said, in his distinctive high-pitched and nasal Irish West Side voice, "is that Internal Affairs, the DA's office, and the New York State attorney general's office all have to speak to you as soon as possible, prior to the grand jury that will be set for next week." Raymond could smell liquor on Tierny's breath.

"Of course," Raymond said. He watched Tierny leave, and knew now he had no choice. He stood up, walked over to the brass serving tray against the wall, and poured himself a glass of water, wondering to himself if he was the best person to send out to talk with 50 reporters.

"Mayor, there's a problem," Raymond said.

The mayor took a deep breath, exhaled, stood up, and said, "What is it?"

"I've known Sheilah for a long time, since I was in narcotics in the '90s and she was an assistant district attorney in the special narcotics court."

"So? What's the deal? Both of you were stealing weight? Using? What? Tell me."

"No," Raymond laughed. "We've been secretly seeing each other for the past three years, and I'm concerned about the grand jury and a possible conflict."

The mayor didn't move. Neither did Raymond. The mayor looked directly at him. Raymond stared back. Finally, the mayor broke the silence. "That's it?"

"That's it."

Brown sat back down, leaned back in his leather executive chair, and broke out in a locker-room grin. "Ray, you're single, as is she. She's gorgeous, smart, and one of the powerful people in the city, and you're the fucking police commissioner and you'd make a great looking couple. I think most people know you guys dated in the '90s when you were both single, and I don't think they'd give a fuck about today, but I get the conflict thing. She's going to have to recuse herself without making it a public spectacle, if you guys want to keep this under wraps."

The grand jury was mandatory when a police officer, even the commissioner, was involved in any homicide, and the district attorney was always the one who represented the state.

The mayor opened the door of his office and motioned for his counsel to come back in the room. Tierny burped as he felt the heaviness in the air. "What's wrong?"

"Well," the mayor said, "we have a little problem here." He laid out the situation for Tierny, who shifted into defense mode.

Tierny looked at Raymond and then back at the mayor. "Who else knows?"

"My chief of staff," Raymond said. Then he added, "And my bodyguard."

"Great," Tierny said sarcastically.

"You don't have to worry about them," Raymond said, hearing how weak he sounded.

"Yes, okay, we'll see. On her side?"

"The only one I'm sure of is her chief of staff, Stephanie Mills."

The mayor frowned as his wheels turned, then spoke directly to Tierny. "Listen, this is fucking stupid. No one's doing anything wrong; it's just a perception issue to avoid conflicts. Sheila will recuse herself from this proceeding, but without making any kind of special announcement. She'll just assign it to her first deputy, Dolores Rhonni. If anybody asks Sheilah why, she can say her mother is sick, her dog died, whatever. I don't care what, but she won't be in charge of this grand jury."

The mayor's face tightened. He put his fists on his hips, lowered his head, and spoke directly now to Raymond. "Rick, from this point forward, not only from a perception perspective, but more importantly an ethical one as well, don't call Dannis, don't email her, don't text her, and I would go as far as saying don't attend any public or private functions where there is any chance at all you will be in the same place. The problem here is that the ethical issue could be blown up in the press and last for a fucking three months, and we don't need that."

The mayor turned back to Tierny: "You speak to Mills. Explain to her why Sheila should recuse herself, which I'm sure they're already thinking about." He paused, then used his hand to gesture to each of them, waving it back and forth. "From this moment forward, no one talks to the press about anything connected to the grand jury." To Raymond: "The sad thing is, that this is juicy enough that the press would forget about this scumbag you killed and you and Dannis would be tabloid headlines for months. Enough of that, Rick; you're going to need outside counsel. The city will represent you at the grand jury, but you'll need a private lawyer to get you through the legal maze. Make sure he's sitting next to you during your interviews with IA, Dolores, or anyone in the the attorney general's office. We need to make sure this flows smoothly without any bumps. You got it?"

"Yes sir," Raymond nodded.

To Tierny: "Get him the best lawyer we have. Call the Corporation Counsel and tell him I want someone he can trust with his life. That's who I want." Tierny scribbled a note to himself on a small spiral pad. "Okay," the mayor said. "Let's get on top of this."

Tierny then said softly, "There are 50 reporters in the Blue Room waiting for a briefing. How are we going to do this?"

There was a knock on the door. "Now what," Brown said as he went to the door and opened it. It was FBI agent Jones. "Good morning, Chelsea," the mayor said; the first-name familiarity came from his knowing her since his days as an assistant U.S. attorney. "What have you got?" the mayor asked.

"It's bad," Jones said. "They found a shitload of extremist propaganda, money, weapons, and other stuff in Paterson linking him to the shooting, but they've also confirmed now that he wasn't acting alone."

"Motherfucker!" Brown blurted out.

"There's more. Turns out Bakheer was a U.S. citizen, born in 1985, only he never really lived here. His father was an Egyptian military officer who came to the States in 1984 for training, stayed until 1986, a year after Bakheer was born. He then brought the boy back to Egypt, where he lived until two years ago. That's when he returned to the States."

"The Bureau didn't have him on their radar?" Raymond said, cutting in and sounding incredulous.

"It's one of the major loopholes of our immigration policy," Jones said. "We call them 'anchor babies' . . . non–U.S. citizens intentionally come to the country so their children will be born citizens. When the child turns 21, he, or she, can, in turn, petition for their parents to become citizens. That's what happened here. Bakheer petitioned for his parents to become U.S. citizens once his father retired from the Egyptian military. The parents spent half the year in Egypt and the other half in the U.S. They've both since passed."

"Go on," the mayor said.

"The two phones we found, one was apparently a burner—a temporary throwaway you can buy in any bodega. He only called one number with it. The FBI ran it, and their report says it led to another burner that communicated daily with seven more phones, bouncing off relays in Paterson, Brooklyn, Detroit, Fayetteville in North Carolina, Las Vegas, and LA. Every one of these lines died as soon as Bakheer went down. Every one. We've determined there are at least six or seven more involved, and we're actively searching for them. This is an ongoing situation."

"That's it," the mayor said. "I'm going to give the press the name of the shooter, which they already have anyway, thanks to that Breshill, and refer them to the district attorney's office, the FBI, and the NYPD's press shack. Okay, let's do this. Rick. Chelsea, you come with me. Let's get this over with."

Rick felt like he was walking into a firing squad.

CHAPTER 5

8:15 pm, Wednesday, 4 October

With the Suburban in the shop, Taylor Shelby was behind the wheel of a blacked-out NYPD Ford Explorer, heading south from Riverdale. WQXR was piping classical music. He hated classical music but it was Raymond's favorite station, and he didn't want to change the station and go through that hurricane. He had on a white tee shirt, dark-blue pressed jeans, black loafers, no socks, and clear-lens prescription glasses. Archer was in the passenger seat wearing the same outfit, making them look like twins.

Rick Raymond was sitting in the back, wearing a light-gray windbreaker, pilot Ray-Bans, a black sweatshirt, khakis, socks, and sneakers. Gallagher was next to him, also dressed down. The traffic wasn't too bad today for rush hour. They sat for nearly a half hour in the nightly East Side bumper-to-bumper crawl to the Ed Koch Bridge until the bottleneck broke. Shelby then sped toward 73rd Street and Madison.

Their destination, the Marcus, was an exclusive Upper East Side boutique hotel, six stories high, all the rooms well-appointed suites. It catered to celebrities, politicians, and a high-end corporate clientele, all of whom were attracted to the Marcus for its no-questions-asked, no-press-allowed policies of privacy. It was sufficiently upscale for those who insisted on luxury, and was necessarily low-key for those who counted on the hotel's policy that what happened with whom at the Marcus stayed inside the suites at the Marcus. Unlike most hotels, the bar was located well off the main entrance, its double doors guarded by a pair of beefy ex-wrestlers. Nobody got past them if the concierge didn't first call ahead. That ensured it would never become a public social gathering place instead of the private convenience it was for its specialized clientele. Rick Raymond and Sheilah Dannis used the hotel for their own personal rendezvous when they didn't feel like driving to Raymond's apartment in the Bronx or her place in Brooklyn. Normally, neither one of them could have afforded their permanently assigned penthouse suite, but what few people knew was that Dannis's now deceased husband, who had been an extremely wealthy Wall Street hedge fund owner, had also been the primary shareholder of that hotel; and when he died six weeks after being diagnosed with a cancerous brain tumor, he'd left his shares of the hotel, plus $137 million in a trust, to his wife. So Sheilah Dannis was not only smart, powerful, and gorgeous; she was filthy rich.

The Explorer drove down the ramp to the hotel's underground lot, and Gallagher and Raymond got out and walked quickly through a short hallway at the rear, to an elevator directly adjacent to the freight elevator. It was marked "Private." Gallagher rang for the elevator, and within 20 seconds its doors opened. The elevator proved to be the same size as the freight elevator, but the inside was covered with deepest, darkest cherry wood, granite railings, and plush carpet, and was lightly scented with lavender from the bouquet that was changed daily. This was the hotel's VIP elevator, and a uniformed employee of the hotel was always on hand to operate it. As he was trained, he did not look directly at either Gallagher or Raymond, nor did he have to ask what floor. He had taken them on this brief vertical journey to the penthouse dozens of times. As always, Gallagher got out first, walked the few steps through the alcove past an open door, where a butler met him and nodded. "Mr. Gallagher, Commissioner, how are you fine gentlemen this evening? Commissioner, I'm so sorry to hear about the officer that died last night."

"Thank you, Nelson. That means a lot."

Nelson, one of the hotel's six VIP butlers, walked Gallagher and Raymond to the apartment, down the pink-walled, softly lit corridor, with its baby blue rugs, to the massive double doors marked "Penthouse A." Gallagher used his own personal plastic key, swung open the door, scanned the room, then handed the key to Raymond and told him that he'd see him in the morning. Gallagher took the main elevator down to the lobby and walked into the bar, where he would nurse a couple of Coca-Colas and munch on bar nuts before heading home.

As he began to undress, Raymond turned on the TV to NY 1, sound off. The mayor was holding another press conference. He clicked on the sound. ". . . and the Transit Authority will have to . . ." He hit mute again. He went to the bar, cracked open a fresh fifth of Dewars, poured himself half a glass, no ice, took a deep swig, smacked his lips as he banged the glass on the counter, walked into the bathroom. He turned on the smaller TV, strapped high on the wall over the sink and conveniently tilted down, again keeping the sound off. The mayor was still talking. Raymond stripped off the rest of his clothes, turned on the shower faucets, waited until the water was the right temperature, and stepped in.

When he was finished, he slipped into the white terry robe hanging on a hook behind the door, wiped the mirror clear with his palm, combed his hair, shaved, and then slapped on a little aftershave the hotel made sure was always in full supply for him. He used it sparingly, not enough to suffocate anyone, just enough to sting. He went to the living room. There was a soft rap on the door. He turned the TV off.

He went to the door, looked through the one-way peephole, then opened the door slowly. Sheilah walked in to the living room. Without saying a word, she took off her beige coat and tossed it and her purse onto the sofa. She headed for the bedroom. Raymond followed. He sat on the side of the bed and watched intensely as Sheilah, having still said nothing, looked away as she reached behind and unzipped her dark-blue dress. She wiggled it into a heap around her shiny black spike heels. She looked statuesque in her black bra, black bikini panties, garter belt, sheer black stockings, and spike heels. Having given him enough time to eat her with his eyes, she came over slowly and sat next to him. He could smell her perfume. She put her arms around his neck while he reached behind and unhooked her bra. She shimmied it off down her arms and let it drop. She put her hands on either side of his head, pulled him forward and buried his face in her breasts. She held him that way until she could feel his face was sufficiently warm. She let him go and he stood up. He opened his robe and let it drop to the floor. She smiled; he was ready.

Sheilah pulled the thick silk bed cover down until it fell off the edge. She then pulled the sheets back. She turned and looked into Raymond's eyes for the first time and smiled as she hooked her thumbs into the top of her panties and pulled them down until they fell to the floor. She stepped out of them, held her hand out; he took it, and she guided him into the bed. She kissed him lightly. He could taste her lipstick. "Good evening, Commissioner," she purred.

He laughed softly. "Good evening, District Attorney." He could hear the after-husk in his own voice.

She slipped beside him, stretched out, and pulled him on top.

Downstairs, in the bar, Gallagher was about to order yet another Coke, when he heard a familiar voice behind him.

"Chief," the voice said. Gallagher turned. It was the reporter, Sammy Breshill. His tie was loosened, his hair was a bit mussed, and his pants, like always, Gallagher thought, needed to be donated to charity.

"What's up, Mr. Breshill?" Gallagher said in the most sarcastic voice he could muster, wondering how he managed to get past the other media marauders at the front entrance.

"Fancy meeting you here," Breshill said, his face turning into something just short of a sneer. Then he added, "Nothin.'"

"They must let anyone in here," Gallagher quipped.

"I've got friends."

"Really? There's a headline you could sell to Ripley."

"Where's the commissioner?

"In Bimini. He wanted to go for a swim."

"With Dannis?"

Gallagher put his fresh, cold Coke down and got off his stool. He was nearly a head taller than Breshill, who remained seated on his stool. "What's that supposed to mean?"

Breshill grinned, his best defensive weapon. "I was just wondering . . . in the midst of all this, and with the grand jury coming up . . ."

Gallagher got in his face. "Stop wondering, and go look for some real news."

Breshill laughed softly as he turned away and took a sip of his drink. He talked without looking back at Gallagher. "Just one question, Jerry. I've got sources in the DA's office that have told me that Dannis will not be handling the GJ. She in Bimini too?"

Gallagher didn't take the bait. "Why don't you ask her?"

"I will," Breshill said, smiling. "When I can find her. She seems to have deserted her office." Breshill finished his drink, got up, and headed for the door. When he was a safe distance from Gallagher, he added, "I hear her First Deputy Rhonni is going to put Raymond on the stand. Something about police brutality." Before Gallagher could say anything, Breshill waved goodbye and left. Gallagher took out a pad and made notes, headed by the time, date, and place.

Raymond checked his watch. He would have to leave soon.

"I didn't bring my clothes, so I'm going to have to head on home. Are you staying here tonight?"

Dannis rolled over and kissed him on his mouth, putting her hand on the side of his face. "I'm going to stay here," she said.

"Okay, I gotta go," he said. "It's nearly 10:30."

"I didn't realize it was that late," she said, and kissed him again. "I'll see you downtown."

"Yeah." He watched her get out of bed, her naked body sticky and slick with sweat. He felt a puff inside, in his stomach. He was about to throw in the towel and stay the night, but the thought of heading up to the Bronx at 5 am just to get fresh clothes changed his mind.

In 15 minutes he was dressed. Dannis was standing by the bed, shoving her stockings, garter belt, and heels into her large blue Vuitton bag that she'd take with her in the morning. She wiped off her make-up with a towelette, and went over to the chest of drawers and pulled out a black sheer negligee that looked like it belonged in a Chanel commercial.

"We're going to have to talk about this grand jury thing," he said to her as she walked him to the door.

"We'll get through it," she said. "It's going to be all right. You didn't do anything wrong. Dolores is good. She'll make it more than clear to the jurors that the homicide was justifiable."

"I'm not worried about any of that."

"Then what?"

"You and me. When the press realizes you're not handling this, they'll get stupid and start asking why . . ."

She didn't let him finish. "There's nothing to find out. My deputy is handling it and that's it. It's not like we're doing anything wrong." She smiled. "Zip your pants up; your beautiful big thing is peeking out." Raymond zipped up. She kissed him lightly on his cheek. "Bye, darling," she whispered, as he slipped out the door.

He left the room and walked down the hallway to the VIP elevator where Nelson appeared within seconds. A few minutes later,

Raymond was walking out the side entrance of the building where Gallagher and Archer were standing outside the Explorer talking. He looked at Gallagher. "What are you still doing here?"

"I was going to leave and then ran into that prick Breshill."

"Where?"

"Here, at the bar. He's snooping around about you and Sheilah."

"Fuck him," Raymond said, as he got into the back of the Explorer. "I'll see you in the morning. Let's go guys . . . head on home.

Archer spoke into the mike in his sleeve, "Eagle One to Eagle Three. We're heading to the Castle."

CHAPTER 6

7:30 am, Thursday, 5 October

Before Raymond arrived every morning, all the New York newspapers were neatly fanned, one atop the other, on one side of his large oak desk in his office on the 14th floor of One Police Plaza in Lower Manhattan. On top was the *New York Herald*, with its banner headline, in full caps and italics, screaming:

POLICE ROAD RAGE?
HERO COMMISSIONER HITS RED LIGHT,
GRAND JURY CONVENED
Story by Sammy Breshill starts on page 3

He picked the paper up and opened it to page 3, read a few lines of the piece, then slammed the paper down on the desk. With his left arm, he pushed the rest of the dailies off his desk into a wastepaper basket that went from empty to full in a millisecond. That Breshill, he thought. He could kill him. A perp kills a cop, shoots another, then shoots another and gets killed while he's in a running gun battle with more cops. Clearly a justifiable homicide; but knowing there's a grand jury being convened, Breshill wanted to make sure there were public questions! Every juror will be familiar with the case; all the papers, the local news, and CNN were playing the brutality up big. Baby, baby, baby, where did your love go?

> *I was standing in front of the world's financial center directing people from my command to assist at the temporary command post, when suddenly I heard this incredibly loud explosion coming from above me. People started to run in all directions, as I looked up to see the top of Tower II beginning to implode. I turned and ran with the others, but there was nowhere to go. I found myself running straight toward one of the buildings. There were these huge, round pillars in front of the buildings, and I could see cops running. I backed up against one pillar as the debris started to fire in all directions. I waited for it to stop. No one could breathe because of the heavy clouds of smoke. Three behind me survived. The ones who'd run in front of me didn't.*

His phone rang. It was the mayor's chief of staff. "Come on over; he wants to see you."

Raymond sighed, got up, checked himself once in the mirror of his private office bathroom, fixed the knot of his tie, and headed for his private elevator. City Hall was across the street. The air had a fall bite to it. Raymond half-trotted across the street, against the light; a lifetime of living in the city had taught him how to instinctively weave between the cars of the slow-moving street traffic. At City Hall, he was waved through the security barricades at the main entrance, and walked down the hall to the left, to Mayor Brown's office. Shelly, the mayor's gatekeeper and administrative assistant, nodded for him to go straight in. The mayor, who was standing, came around his desk, shook hands with Raymond, and offered him a cup of coffee. Raymond nodded yes, and Brown rang for Shelly to bring them two fresh cups, cream and sugar on the side.

"That what you wanted to see me about? A coffee break?"

The mayor sat back down and gestured for Raymond to take a seat on the other side of the desk. "Seen the morning papers?"

"They were on my desk when I got in. That prick Breshill."

"Yeah, well, I don't want him, you, or it spilling over on me, with reelection coming up next year." Shelly brought in a silver tray with a coffeepot, two cups and saucers, a bowl of sugar cubes, and a chilled filled creamer. She knew by now they both liked it the same way, two lumps and a splash of cream. She left without saying a word.

"Everyone knows you're not, but he's trying to make you a target," Brown said.

"Clearly. And everyone who reads the papers or watches TV knows it."

The mayor took a sip of his coffee, holding the cup and saucer close to his face. "How in the fuck is he trying to turn this into police brutality." He put his coffee on his desk. "Is there something we're missing? Something that has a lot of unexpected curves he can throw right over the plate? Like on an icy mountain road, that kind of curve can throw you over without any warning." He took another sip of his coffee. "I guess we're lucky; a grand jury is a closed session. No judge, no reporters, just the DA, a jury, and you. I know Dolores will not be looking for an indictment and the use of force was justified, but anything can happen in the grand jury, especially when some obnoxious juror starts asking questions."

"It will be fine," Raymond said, finishing his cup. "Dolores is tough, but regardless of what is asked by the grand jurors, she's not looking for an indictment. She's putting forward the investigative facts to justify the homicide. The most liberal of attorneys couldn't argue the justification."

"Let's hope," Brown said. "I don't like Breshill pushing this road rage police brutality shit and creating questions. I know it sells papers, but it also sometimes drives prosecutors, and we need this to go away quietly. What's up with the sling?"

"Probably just a sprain; it's okay."

"Keep it on through the grand jury. And for God's sake, stay away from Sheilah until this is all over."

Three nights later, having arrived in separate cars, Raymond and Sheilah were having dinner in a small Connecticut seafood house 30 miles northeast of the city. Raymond had arranged for them to have a private room, curtained off from the main dining room. They each had a vodka martini, topped with a trio of three black olives speared across their glasses like an African safari kill. Sheilah took the first one in her mouth and pulled the toothpick slowly out. Raymond yanked all three off the pick with his fingers and shoved them in his mouth all at once, like they were popcorn. When he could speak again, he said, "What's the latest on the grand jury?"

"I'd guess pretty good. The perp had a gun out; you were defending yourself. That's your defense and what you will say on the stand."

"There were a lot of cops there."

"Good. Not a single one will testify against you. They'll all praise you like you were Gandhi."

"Let's hope."

"The grand jury will call you as a witness, not as a defendant, but you're always a big fish, remember that. You will be one of several witnesses they'll call. Shelby, for sure. And Archer. They're the primary focus, especially Shelby, since he was driving, but no one in that room will be interested. They always look at the big enchilada."

She stopped talking when the waiter came through the curtain, pad out, head down. They ordered crispy-skinned branzino with roasted almonds, creamed spinach, a bowl of well-done french fries, and a bottle of California sauterne. The waiter said softly, "Very good" and backed out through the curtain.

She continued: "It's the DA's agenda that is pushed on the grand jury. You know the old saying, 'You can indict a ham sandwich,' but in order for them to come back with a true bill of indictment, you have to have a strong case against the person who killed the pig. There's a big leap from a grand jury to an indictment, especially when the key witness is a national hero. Your only caution flag is the police brutality nonsense the press is trying to build into something. No one in the DA's office can or will make that case, unless the court of public opinion becomes overwhelming; then they won't be able not to."

"Then what?" Raymond asked, draining his martini.

"It won't happen. Dolores isn't stupid. She knows it's all bullshit."

"You're sure of that?"

Sheilah smiled. "I'm sure. Even though the mayor has nothing to do with the DA, and absolutely no influence over us, I know he wants you in and out of there as quickly as possible—and Dolores likes her job, and I need funding for my office. But really, we're beating a dead horse. There's nothing to this. I think the mayor's making you crazy because he's up for reelection."

Their food came, and the wine. The waiter deboned the branzino as they sipped the sauterne, and then they ate, mostly in silence. For dessert, they shared a wedge of tiramisu and had two cups of coffee. The waiter brought the check, and Raymond paid in cash. They got up, but left separately, Sheilah going first; her driver pulled her car up to the front door of the restaurant within seconds after she stepped outside. Raymond followed 10 minutes later, and his car did the same, Archer stepping out to open the back door to let him in.

Neither Sheilah nor Raymond had noticed the small man sitting at the far end of the bar, hunched over a glass of beer. As soon as Raymond went through the front door of the restaurant, the man stood, still holding his beer, and moved to the edge of the large window that looked directly onto the driveway. Breshill watched Raymond get into his car and pull away in the direction of the New

England Thruway. He then went back to the bar, took out his small spiral pad from the back pocket of his pants, and started jotting down notes.

Breshill recorded everything about the dinner, including the time, the place, even what they had eaten. From his perch, he had been able to see the trays of food as they were brought to the private room.

He threw a twenty onto the bar, shoved the receipt into his pocket so he could get reimbursed by the paper, and headed for self-parking at the rear of the restaurant.

Charging for a valet would be pushing it with his editor.

CHAPTER 7

5:45 am, Wednesday, 11 October

DA DALLIANCE WITH COMMISSIONER BEFORE GRAND JURY

Story by Sammy Breshill starts on page 3

Raymond read the article as he finished his coffee, knowing that everyone in the city had seen it by now. It implied that Sheilah had gone to an out-of-town dinner with a certain "higher-up" in the police department, and wondered if it had had anything to do with her not being in charge of Commissioner Raymond's upcoming grand jury appearance. Breshill had stepped up to the plate, but hadn't taken a swing, Raymond thought. Maybe he was waiting for the next day's edition.

Raymond knew that the mayor had read it too. I'm going to kill this motherfucker, he thought to himself. The mayor had told him to stay away from the DA until the conclusion of the grand jury, and although there was nothing wrong with them meeting, it was the perception of an impropriety that would drive the press. That in turn would drive the mayor crazy and cause problems between him and the mayor.

The rule is referred to as the 180; that is, 180 hours, 1 week (7.5 days), after a crime is committed, except in rare circumstances, a grand jury must be convened. Eighteen jurors are seated, and it is up to them to either bring a bill of indictment or not. In this instance, the grand jury would conduct an investigation into the death of Samir Abdullah Bakheer, caused by Shelby, Archer, and Raymond, and determine whether the killing was justified or not.

On the morning of Wednesday, October 11, the grand jury began its work. The steps leading up to the courthouse were jammed with onlookers, TV reporters and their cameramen, print media. Everyone and his fucking sister, Raymond thought to himself, all of them focused on him, like he had just discovered the cure for cancer, or killed the guy who did. And there, right at the front of the pack, was Sammy Breshill, holding his pad and pencil, ready to take down anything he might be able to use for the next edition. The good thing, Raymond knew, was that the press was not allowed inside the courtroom while the grand jury was in session. Nobody extraneous, not even other witnesses. Raymond could see both Archer and Shelby trotting up the steps, not together, and Dolores coming up the other side, surrounded by reporters, mikes thrust in her face. Cannibals, Rick thought to himself. Fucking goddamn cannibals. And the chief headhunter, he believed, was Breshill, who was looking to make a holiday barbecue out of him. Something had to be done about him, Raymond thought to himself, and he would get it done. As soon as this grand jury thing was behind him.

Raymond was huddled in the courthouse hallway with Archer and Shelby, until, at 10:52, the court clerk came out and called

Raymond's name. He was going to be the first to testify. "Here," Raymond said.

"Follow me, please," the court clerk said, gesturing with his hand for him to follow.

The grand jury room was large, with 18 jurors seated triple-tiered. An empty seat was placed opposite them. To the jurors' left, at an angle, was a large oak desk. Seated there was Dolores, with a sheaf of papers in front of her, a pitcher of water, a glass at one side, two pencils and a pad on the other. Raymond was sworn in and was seated directly facing the jury, at which time he was told that everything he said could be used at a trial. Seated next to Dolores was an assistant DA from the office, there to observe the proceedings. There was no judge.

Dolores, dressed in a gray suit, a white shirt buttoned to the top, a long skirt, dark sheer stockings, and high-heeled black shoes, stood and came around to the front of the table. Raymond flashed on how good-looking she was, then pushed that out of his brain. He had enough troubles, he thought to himself.

Dolores began. "State your name, please."

"Richard Raymond."

"Occupation?"

"I am the police commissioner for the city of New York."

"How long have you held this position, Mr. Raymond?"

"Eighteen months. Just over eighteen months."

"And how did you get to be commissioner?"

Raymond shifted in his seat and noticed, for the first time, how warm it was in the room. "I was appointed by the mayor of the city of New York."

"So this was a political appointment."

"No. Yes. It was a job the mayor felt I was best suited for." Raymond let a slight smile come over his face. "I'd like to think I was the best person for the job." What was she doing, Raymond wondered? Why go there?

"What did you do before you became commissioner?"

Rick turned away from Dolores and looked beyond her, directly at the jury. "I was a member of the New York City police force close to 30 years." There was a sense of satisfaction in his voice.

"Where did you train to be a policeman?"

He looked back at Dolores. "I have a bachelor's degree from John Jay University of Criminal Justice in New York City, and a master's in business administration from St. John's University in Queens.

Dolores took a few steps forward, positioning herself at an angle where she could see both Raymond and the jurors. "Have you ever been involved in a police action where you killed a suspect?"

The air in the room got even hotter. He felt the collar of his white shirt get wet and tighten against his throat. He wanted to loosen his tie and open the top button, but didn't. "Yes, I have," he said, deliberately.

"More than once?"

"Yes."

"Did you use your weapon?"

"On two separate occasions. Both times with battle-seasoned veterans with me. Once in 1989 and once in 1991. Both events involved narcotics. Both suspects had weapons. Both fired their weapons at me, and when I returned fire I killed them. I had to make a split-second decision and felt that deadly force was needed. I did what I thought I had to do. In case you haven't noticed, there's a war going on out on the street, and we are your best and last protection in that war."

Dolores took a beat, then said evenly, "Just answer my questions, please." She then walked back to her desk, turned a few pages of her sheaf, took a pen out just to hold in her hand, looked up, and began firing questions at Raymond that effectively laid out the story of how Bakheer was killed:

"Commissioner Raymond, were you in an NYPD Suburban with Detectives Archer and Shelby in the early morning hours of October 4, 2017?"

"Yes I was."

"Did there come a time that you heard a radio message by dispatch saying that there was a running gun battle in the area of 125th Street and Broadway?"

"Yes ma'am, I did."

"And what if anything did you tell Detective Shelby when you heard that transmission?"

"I ordered him to exit the Westside Highway at 125th Street and head toward the suspect, and he did. As we came off 125th and were heading toward Broadway, we saw a number of police officers on foot in pursuit of the suspect, whom I personally witnessed turn and fire on the pursuing officers."

"And what happened then?"

"Detective Shelby hit the suspect, as did a second responding unmarked police unit."

"Commissioner, did you order Detective Shelby to hit the suspect with the vehicle he was driving?"

Raymond hesitated a minute, wondering if it were a trick question, and then answered, "Yes I did. I felt that our lives and the lives of the responding cops were in danger, so I gave the order to hit the suspect." As Raymond finished the sentence, he looked at the grand jurors, all 18 of whom were staring at him with their mouths open, appearing shell-shocked.

Quickly glancing at the jurors, Dolores didn't miss a beat. She continued, "So you ordered Shelby to hit the suspect, which resulted in Bakheer's death?"

"Yes ma'am."

"And you believe, given the circumstances, that the use of deadly force, the vehicle, was justified?"

"Yes, I do."

"Thank you, Commissioner. Let's take a five-minute break," Dolores said. The jurors filed out to their private area, several of them desperate for a cigarette. When the jury reconvened, Dolores asked if anyone had any questions for Raymond, normal procedure in a grand jury.

One juror stood up. He was tall, salt-and-pepper hair, dressed like a lawyer in an I'm-a-tough-litigator suit. "I think we would all like to know why the district attorney is not handling this case?"

Dolores turned to Raymond, like she was looking for an answer, and then turned back to the juror. "That is not an appropriate question for this witness. I am representing the district attorney and conducting this investigation. Commissioner Raymond cannot speak for the DA or our office."

Dolores turned to Raymond and said. "You are excused, Mr. Raymond. You are instructed not to discuss your testimony with anybody." Raymond stood and was escorted by the clerk to the door. He left the courtroom, past the other witnesses waiting to be called, without saying a word or looking directly at them, and headed outside, knowing he was walking into a lion's den of media. He took a deep breath and steeled himself against what would be a cacophony of shouted questions, shoved microphones, overzealous reporters.

"Mr. Commissioner, are you dating the district attorney?" No answer.

He spotted Breshill in the crowd and deliberately walked right in front of him. "How often do you stay in uptown hotels, Mr. Commissioner?" Breshill shouted. Raymond stared long and hard at the reporter, but said nothing.

There was a distinct chill in the fall air. He buttoned two buttons on his coat and decided to walk back to headquarters.

Only then did he realize his entire shirt was soaking wet, all the way down to his jockeys.

CHAPTER 8

1:05 pm, Wednesday, 11 October

Back in his office, Raymond changed into a clean white shirt, poured himself a fresh cup of coffee, kissed the air as he took the first hot sip, then poured himself a glass of water to cool off his mouth. He believed he had done well, except for that last asshole juror who thought it was his moral duty to drill down on why Sheilah wasn't handling the case for the city. Must be a lawyer, Raymond thought to himself. Anyway, he was glad it was over, and the sooner Dolores finished with the rest of the witnesses, most of whom were cops, the sooner this thing would be over and past him. Dolores, he thought, was no slouch; she had done a masterful job, even had him going for a while, but the way she finished, he had to be in the clear.

He glanced down at the neatly stacked pink message slips on his desk. He riffled through them, the way a teller does stacks of dollar bills. One from Sheilah, of course, but probably not the best idea to call her back before the GJ decision comes down. Then, he thought, Jesus, they're making me act like I'm guilty!

And one from Breshill. *Breshill! That* prick! A real ballbuster, looking to bust mine and elevate himself by instigating bad chatter about me and Sheilah. I'd like to call him in here and slap him around, even if it meant another grand jury. It'd be worth it, he chuckled softly to himself. But not necessary. He knew how to handle flies like Breshill without him even knowing he was being handled. When all of this dies down . . .

The desk phone rang, cutting into his thoughts. He picked it up. "Chelsea Jones from the FBI on line 1," Janey said. Janey was his assistant/receptionist/coffeemaker/call screener/confidant. His work wife. She had started as an intern in Raymond's office 10 years earlier when he was an inspector, to earn extra credit, and after graduation from John Jay College of Criminal Justice, accepted Raymond's offer to stay on full-time. Recently she got a bug up her ass to become a lawyer, so now she was a first-year law student, attending NYU at night.

Raymond clicked on line 1. "Chelsea, how are you?"

"Good. You?"

"Getting along."

"We have a problem," Jones said. Raymond's first thought was that it had something to do with the grand jury.

"What's that?"

"I can't talk about it on the phone." Raymond's stomach did a somersault. Jones continued, "I'll be there in 15 minutes" and hung up.

Raymond sat in his chair and stared at the big wall clock until he heard the door to the outer office open.

On Janey's instructions, Jones went directly into Raymond's office, pushing open the door and entering with her FBI-confident stride. She had on a dark-blue FBI windbreaker with the zipper open, a white shirt, tan belt with a silver buckle, tan khakis, dark-blue knit socks, and orthopedic shoes. Out of sight behind her jacket, her holstered Glock 23 was hooked to her belt. Raymond got up and came around the desk to shake hands with her. "Coffee? Water?"

"No," Jones said. Raymond gestured for her to sit down in one of the big beige leather chairs. He sat in the other.

Jones asked, "Heard anything from your sister's kid these days?"

"Jimmy? He's doing great. Matter of fact, I just sent him and a team of our guys down to Fayetteville, North Carolina, on an investigation, something we believe is related to the Times Square shooting."

Jimmy Kerrigan was the son of Raymond's sister Linda. He was an NYPD detective, assigned to the New York FBI Joint Terrorism Task Force. Whenever an investigation starts in the Southern District of New York, no matter where it leads, these detectives follow, because they know all the background on the original case. There were New York City police detectives all over the country, and in a dozen foreign countries. Jimmy had been pulled to Fayetteville to work with the Feds there, in case anything turned up that had a connection back to Times Square.

"He's a fine boy," Jones said.

"Yes. I hear the guys in North Carolina really like him, even if he is from New York," Raymond joked.

Jones laughed politely. "Keep me posted." Then she changed the subject: "Any word yet about your GJ?"

Raymond's chest tightened. "I'm waiting now. I think it went well."

"Good." Jones paused, then gestured with her right hand as she spoke, as if drawing a picture of what she was saying. "Okay, listen up. You're going to hear about this shortly from your people, but I want it to come from me first. I think we're back up on the cell leader for Bakheer. We now believe, while in Paterson, Bakheer received his orders from one guy out of Detroit; we also believe we have the head guy's phone number and the four other phones still calling in to him. The reason I'm telling you all this is because one of those phones is in Brooklyn, and it seems like whoever it is, he's planning something here. He could also lead us back to the cell leader in Detroit. We want him."

"So do I, yesterday. These guys are dangerous."

"You have no idea. Listen, Rick, our analysts believe they're up to something big, right here in the city."

Raymond didn't know what to say.

Jones continued, "We just got word from one of our sources that there is a shitload of chatter that says that a major attack is coming. Our cyber guys are picking up bits and pieces on the dark web. We believe there are two, maybe three suicide bombers involved. We have two under surveillance, but aren't sure of their real identities yet, and we're missing the third guy."

"Holy shit . . ."

"It gets worse. I'm waiting for word from our people, but the guy up on the wires, the wiretaps, believes the third player is one of yours. We believe the third player is one of yours."

Raymond stared at Jones for a long time before speaking in measured tones. "What are you talking about?"

Jones continued, still mapping out her story with her hands, like a conductor doing Mozart. "We were on a wire on the guy from Detroit, and these two guys begin calling in from Brooklyn. Of course, we're now on their phones. Yesterday they spoke about 'an Osama-size spectacular event.' They said someone living in Brooklyn, who lives near one of their other contacts in Brooklyn and attends the same mosque, is holding their stash of weapons and explosives. The guy in Detroit asked them how they're going to get their arsenal to the site, and he said 'Brooklyn' had clearance and no one would stop him."

"Reliable?"

"It's them talking; that's pretty reliable. Besides being up on their phones, we have two different informants in the Brooklyn mosque, and both independently advised us that there are four or five New York City cops that pray there. Both of them told us, separately, that they've seen one cop, specifically, hanging out with a few new characters that recently started attending the mosque, but they don't know the cop's name or identity, and we don't want to raise up the imam at the mosque by asking questions."

"When are they planning to hit?"

"They said, 'The heavens will open up at 4 pm on Friday.'"

"This Friday?"

"Correct."

"Jesus, there's no time; this is Wednesday," Raymond said, leaning forward.

"No," Jones said, "there's not enough time to stop them unless we find out who the dirty cop is. We will stay close through Friday's afternoon prayer. They're supposed to meet for lunch after, which should be around 2 pm. We figure the three are going to meet the fourth, the cop, at lunch, and that's when he'll give them their equipment. He may take part in the actual attack, or he may just send them off to do the dirty work and stay back to wait for a new contact from another cell. Either way, he's the key to stopping the attack. We've got to find him before this thing goes down."

The commissioner felt like his head was about to explode. Even if they caught the bastard, the implications of a cop being in on it would be devastating to the department, the city, and the country. There were dozens of honest Muslim employees in the NYPD, hardworking dedicated public servants whose lives would surely be in danger. There could be mobs demanding their heads on silver platters made in America. Raymond knew he had to find out who the cop was and stop the attack before any of the conspiracy reached the public.

Jones told Raymond that the FBI operations center would be live at eight the next morning, with the Joint Terrorism Task Force and members of the NYPD's major case squad involved as well. Everyone who could breathe would be called in on this. Jones continued, explaining how the process would work. "Every private-sector camera will feed into the police and FBI joint operations center, and there will be a dozen surveillance teams, four to six agents each, a counterassault team, or CAT, on standby, and a full load of the NYPD's ESUs—emergency service units. I'll see you bright and early in the morning. We will do all we can and leave the rest in God's hands."

Raymond nodded. "I'll be there," he said. They stood and shook hands before Jones left the office. Raymond immediately called the mayor's direct line.

"Yes?"

"Mayor, I've got to see you. It's urgent. I'm on my way."

The mayor could hear something in Raymond's voice he didn't like. "Okay, I'm here."

Raymond put on his jacket and opened the door to his office; four bodyguards and Gallagher were hanging around in reception. Janey was at her desk, where one of the four had been bending over to talk to her. He couldn't help trying to glance at the front of her blouse. They all jumped to attention. Raymond frowned, looked at Gallagher, and nodded for him to follow. Gallagher snapped to Shelby to get to the car, and Archer ran ahead to get the commissioner's private elevator. "I need to see the mayor," Raymond said, as Gallagher held open the elevator door.

Archer lifted his wrist so that he could speak into the small black microphone attached to his sleeve. "Eagle One to Eagle Three, the commissioner is leaving the nest, headed to City Hall. We're 10 minutes out."

The doors closed behind them and opened again in the garage. Raymond's new Suburban was running, with both rear doors opened. Raymond jumped in behind Archer, and Gallagher behind Shelby. When all the doors closed, Shelby gunned it toward the up ramp into the bustling city that Raymond was now desperately trying to save from being blown to hell, and he had zero minus 48 to do it.

CHAPTER 9

3:10 pm, Wednesday, 11 October

Raymond and Gallagher arrived just after three at the mayor's office. Brown was waiting for them. Raymond told Gallagher to wait in reception, then sat down and filled the mayor in on what was going down.

"Jesus," Brown said. "What are you going to do?"

"We're going to stop it."

"How?"

"I don't know yet. I'm going to go along with FBI agent Jones tomorrow and see what we can do. There's one more thing."

"What?"

"We think there could be a dirty cop in on this."

Brown dropped his head, then looked up. "Jesus Christ, are you kidding me? Rick, get the bastard!"

"I'm going to give it my best."

CHAPTER 10

7:35 am, Thursday, 12 October

Raymond arrived at the FBI headquarters, 26 Federal Plaza, in Downtown Manhattan. He and Gallagher were escorted by two agents, who took them in a keyed elevator to the eighth floor. "You stay with me," the commissioner said to Gallagher. The doors opened to a warehouse-sized operations center, dark, with wall lights continually blinking on and off and three dozen desk computers monitored by agents. Each of their screens corresponded to giant ones hung around the walls of the center. An FBI agent walked Raymond and Gallagher over to Jones, who was huddled with a dozen FBI executives and NYPD Deputy Inspector Mickie Tarquette, the commander of the JTTF for the NYPD. Jones turned and introduced the two newcomers to the others.

Raymond shook hands with everyone, and gave a quick shoulder-grip hug to Tarquette, one of the rising stars of the NYPD. They had known each other a long time, going all the way back to when they were both doing patrol. Raymond was a lieutenant when they first met, and they had hit it off from the get-go. With his bushy mop of blond hair, Tarquette looked at least 10 years younger than his 40, and still had the body of an athlete in his prime. Because of his long record of achievement, Raymond had transferred Tarquette to JTTF 10 months earlier, where he was quickly promoted to deputy inspector, one rank above captain. The commanding officer of JTTF was one of the most coveted positions in the NYPD, and Tarquette had sent his request for the assignment directly to Raymond, who was happy to give his approval. It was not only great for the force; it also reflected well on Raymond.

It was about 4:45 pm, just about seven hours since the first plane hit the North Tower. By now, both towers had come down. Four hours earlier, I had confirmed that the plane carrying my wife, Mary, had crashed in Shanksville, PA. The senior brass on the job came to see me personally, to tell me and allow me to leave, but I couldn't. I needed something to occupy my mind, and there was nothing I could do to bring Mary back. As I stood in the rubble wondering what the hell had happened, I felt like my entire world was collapsing. Then, I got a call to report to the auditorium at headquarters. When I arrived, I saw dozens of families of police officers gathered there. At the same time, the police commissioner, the first deputy, and the chief of department entered the room. The police commissioner sat with the family members and spoke with them, and then spoke to everyone, informing them that as of this moment 23 members of the department were missing, and the entire force was going to do everything in its power to find them. The police commissioner looked at me and told the families in the room that my wife had been killed on one of the planes, yet I chose to be there with them. I could see he was trying to be optimistic for the group of family members, but having just come from what was now known as Ground Zero, I knew that the chances of finding them alive at this point were slim to none. Everything and anything not made of steel had been either crushed beyond recognition or vaporized. At that point, I was inspired and motivated to be there for those families. There was nothing I could do for myself and my own loss, but I felt obligated to be there for them.

With Tarquette at his side, Jones briefed the commissioner and Gallagher. "We've been up on two of these guys since we last met on Wednesday. Since then, there were three calls from the Detroit leader, and we're sure, although they speak cryptically and in deep code, that D-day hits at 4 pm."

As they stood talking, an agent's voice came over the notification orders loudspeaker: "We believe that the targets may have arrived at the mosque."

Everybody's attention went to one of the huge monitors, as one camera focused on two men standing outside the mosque and caught one speaking to the other for less than 15 seconds. The one spoken to then walked away, took out his cell phone, and punched in a number. There were no mikes, so no one at headquarters could hear what was being said, and the cameras couldn't pick up the number he dialed. A report quickly came in that it was a new phone, one they had no information for.

"Who is that guy?" Tarquette screamed, pointing at the screen. "Somebody get on that guy! Get his photo to all our surveillance teams and tell them not to let him out of their sight! We need that phone he's on and the number he just called!"

The target hailed a taxi. He got in, and the driver took off. NYPD detective Jeremy Myers, in plain clothes, and FBI agent Clark Coles, sitting in a parked, unmarked car three blocks away, were waiting as the taxi went by. They pulled out, and when they were five blocks from the mosque, the detective hit his rotators and flicked on the siren. "What the fuck are you doing!" the FBI agent said.

"Follow my lead," the detective said, as he pulled the taxi over.

The detective got out of the car and, with gun drawn, standing to the left of the taxi's trunk, ordered both the driver and the passenger in the back seat out of the vehicle. He then put both spread eagle, one on the side of the rear trunk, and one on the opposite side.

"What's going on?" the Haitian cab driver asked, his voice trembling with fright.

"There's been a robbery," the detective said. He had them empty their pockets and put everything, including their phones, on the hood. He then had both sit on the curb while he went through their personal belongings and searched the car. He took the passenger's cell phone and, with his own phone, he snapped shots of the last 10 numbers called. He then got on his radio and spoke into it softly, asking for one of the surveillance teams to put a female agent in the back of one of their cars and drive by, stop, and come up to him, saying she was the victim of the robbery. Three minutes later a car pulled up with a blond female agent in the back passenger seat. Detective Myers walked over, opened the door, asked her to step out, and pointed to the two men. "Are they the ones who robbed you?" he asked her.

She looked at both intently, then back at the detective. She saw the very subtle head shake that told her how to answer. "No, officer," the agent finally said, "I've never seen either of them before." She looked into the detective's eyes, searching for approval of her performance.

"Are you sure, ma'am?"

"I'm positive. They're not the guys."

"Thank you." Detective Myers put her back into the car, closed the door, and watched the car drive off. He then walked over to the two men and apologized, shaking their hands and saying they were cleared and free to go. Eager to get out of there, they picked up their belongings from the roof of the cab, got into the car, and the driver took off.

The detective and FBI agent Coles got back into their car, where Myers called in the photographed numbers to their operations center. Within minutes, the FBI had the name of NYPD officer Victor Hamadi, a uniformed cop out of the Four-One, up in the Bronx. Raymond and his team quickly discovered that Friday was his last tour of duty on the 11–7 overnight shift.

The Friday afternoon prayers ended precisely at two o'clock. The two targets were the first to come out of the mosque. Surveillance cameras followed them down to Atlantic Avenue, where they walked into a small Arab restaurant. They sat down, and quickly another man already in the restaurant joined them at their table. Because his back was facing the door, surveillance wasn't able to make him. The Bureau sent in an Arab agent, who sat at the counter and ordered a bowl of soup. From there, he was able to get a good look at the third man's face and take several photos from his lapel camera. He took a few spoonfuls of soup, put some money on the counter, and left. Once outside and halfway down the street, he said into his wrist mike, "The guy isn't Hamadi." As he continued to walk away, surveillance watched the two targets and the third man get into a minivan parked by a meter at the opposite corner.

The agent got back into his surveillance car. On orders, he began to tail the minivan, careful to keep far enough away so as not to be spotted, but close enough to make sure he didn't lose the targets. He was soon joined by a caravan, each relieving the one before it, to further disguise the tail. They followed the minivan over the Brooklyn Bridge and onto the FDR Drive, heading north. It exited at 42nd Street, near the United Nations, then turned up First Avenue. It made a left on 51st Street headed west. Just as the tail crossed Third Avenue, they saw a man standing in the middle of the street, 100 feet west of the 17th Precinct. One of the NYPD sergeants in surveillance made him as Hamadi, and screamed over the radio, "Target three is just west of the One-Seven! *Stand by!*"

The van slowed a few feet in front of Hamadi. The tail pulled over in front of a hydrant, a half block behind. They watched as

Hamadi went over to his own car, parked less than 100 feet from the One-Seven, opened his trunk, and pulled out two large duffel bags. The side door of the minivan slid open, and Hamadi shoved the bags in. Just before the minivan's door slid closed, he reached into his waistband, pulled out what looked like a semiautomatic hand-gun, and handed it to one of the two targets. Hamadi then reached behind his back, under his coat, pulled out another handgun, and handed that over as well. The door slid shut, and the minivan took off. Hamadi then got back to his car and sat in it, to make sure there was no tail.

Another surveillance car picked up the van as it continued west on 51st Street and then made a left onto Fifth Avenue, a one-way headed south. The van pulled over to the left lane and came to a stop in front of St. Patrick's Cathedral. One female surveillance agent posted at the 50th Street side of the church entered through that door, then stuck her head out one of the doors of the main Fifth Avenue entrance. She saw the van, stepped back in, and reported what she had observed. Over her radio, she said, "Driver is staying put in the front seat. Targets one and two remain in the back of the van. They're wearing some kind of vests; I couldn't see clearly enough; could be a bulletproof vest or bomb vest." She paused, and another voice, from a surveillance vehicle parked on the opposite side of Fifth Avenue, picked it up. "They're definitely putting something under long black coats they're now wearing. I see a gun. Repeat, I see a long gun . . . The van is moving; repeat, the van is moving . . ."

The minivan went to the corner and turned left, toward Madison Avenue. Seven surveillance cars followed as the van next turned left onto Madison, headed north, and made another left at 51st Street, this time driving straight across to Fifth Avenue and stopping adjacent to Rockefeller Center, which was packed with tourists. The van pulled to the left and came to a halt. Two cars from the surveillance caravan had no choice but to pass the van, and then pulled over about 200 feet west of the van toward the Avenue of the Americas. The rest of the caravan turned left on Fifth, pulled over to the right, and the cops and agents jumped out of the cars, scurrying through the Channel Gardens area of Rockefeller Center, disappearing in the crowds.

FBI and NYPD snipers and spotters had been dispatched to the surrounding buildings in Rockefeller Center earlier that morning. The shooters lay flat, the barrels of their sniper rifles invisible as they peeked out from their positions and aimed directly at the van.

The driver of the van just sat there, looking around, while in the back seat, targets two and three adjusted their black coats. The minivan door suddenly swung open, and the two men jumped out into the middle of the street. One of the targets had an AK-47 visible alongside his leg.

Every radio suddenly screamed with an FBI agent's voice: "Target in possession of an AK-47. I repeat, target in possession of an AK-47!"

Jones's voice came on the radio: "Do not, I repeat, do not let them get inside Rock Center." A loudspeaker from a black van parked 20 yards ahead of the minivan blared, "This is the police. Do not move. Drop your weapons and do not move!"

Targets one and two froze momentarily, enough time for what appeared to be an FBI SWAT team and members of the NYPD emergency service unit to materialize out of what seemed like nowhere, machine guns up and ready. An agent screamed for the two to drop their weapons. In response, target one yelled, *"Allahu Akbar!"* and raised his AK-47. Both targets were torn nearly in two by a hail of bullets, their body parts shredded from their torsos. Before their bodies hit the ground, a massive, earsplitting explosion went off, fracturing the minivan into millions of pieces of metal and shrapnel that flew like high-powered bullets everywhere, blowing windows out of buildings. People everywhere began screaming, and the dozens of cops and agents closing in were dropped. The eyes of the lead agent, the one who had yelled for the targets to drop their weapons, were blown out of his head, and smoke poured from the sockets of the skull that had rolled into the street. A few seconds later, there was another bigger and louder explosion.

The rest of the cops and FBI poured out of their vehicles and ran toward what was left of targets one and two.

Raymond and Jones had been watching all of it from headquarters. As Midtown turned into a war zone, Raymond suddenly screamed to no one in particular, "*Where the fuck is Hamadi?*"

CHAPTER 11

5:30 pm, Friday, 13 October

Raymond, Jones, and Gallagher arrived at the mayor's office along with a number of senior NYPD and FBI executives for the press conference, ahead of the start of the local and national news cycles that were about to dominate the airwaves. Local programming had already been suspended in favor of full coverage, and all the cable news networks were in overdrive. The mayor poured them all coffee, tea, or water, whatever their preference, and they sat.

"Okay, what do we have?" the mayor asked Raymond.

"This was a terrorist attack," Raymond began, "thwarted by the NYPD and FBI. Three terrorist were killed, one FBI agent was killed, and two FBI agents and three police officers were injured by debris from the blast and, as it stands now, are still hospitalized. We think this may have been related to the Times Square cop killing, and it could have been much worse had it not been for the men and women of the FBI and NYPD."

"Good. That will begin it. Any news on the dirty cop?"

"We have a team looking for him, and we hope to have him today."

"Have you seen this?" Brown picked up a copy of the afternoon extra edition of the *New York Herald*. The banner read:

TERRORIST ATTACK HITS MIDTOWN
MAYOR AND COMMISSIONER CAUGHT FLAT-FOOTED
Story by Sammy Breshill starts on page 3

And the headline beneath was:

COMMISSIONER AND DA HAVING SECRET RENDEZVOUS?
Story by Sammy Breshill starts on page 5

Raymond looked at it and threw the paper on the sofa directly across from him. "Why don't they just call it the *New York Herald-Breshill*?"

"Rick, I'm up for reelection next year."

"Look, the guy hates you, and he uses me to hurt you. This whole thing about Sheilah and me is nothing more than tabloid gossip. We're both single and can see anyone we want, and the whole impropriety thing with the grand jury is bullshit."

"I know that, and you know that," said the mayor, "but the general public doesn't know that, and that's the problem. The faster the grand jury is concluded, the better. It's less for him to focus on!" Raymond nodded his head as if to say, I understand.

The mayor asked, "Are we ready for the press conference? There must be 200 reporters out there."

"I'm ready," Raymond said.

"Okay," the mayor said. "Let's do this."

The press room was packed with so many reporters, a second anteroom had to be set up, with monitors feeding live what went on in the main room. As the mayor and Raymond walked to the podium, followed by Jones and several other officials, the low rumble in the room quieted.

The mayor, as always, spoke first. "Thank you, ladies and gentlemen. As you know, this has been a terrible day in our great city, but not a completely tragic one. This is not another 9/11, thanks mostly to the men and women of the NYPD and our federal partners, primarily the FBI, which is represented here today by agent Chelsea Jones. They have been working tirelessly on this case, ever since the murders of our good police in Times Square, and the subsequent apprehension of the shooter. We will continue to do everything necessary to protect our great city." There was a round of mild applause that brought a stiff smile to Brown's face. "I'd like to introduce the police commissioner, who will fill you in on the latest events."

The mayor stepped away and gestured for Raymond to step in front of the bank of mikes. "Thank you, everybody. Today's attack, as horrible as it was, was not as bad as it could have been. We are sad to report that an FBI agent was killed in today's attack, two agents and three police officers were injured by the blast, and three civilians were slightly hurt, but other than that, the greatest damage was done to the minivan, its driver who was instantly killed, and the two terrorists who came out shooting. We believe they intended to drive their van into the heart of Rockefeller Center, entering on 51st Street, just beyond the skating rink, to do the most damage. I want to congratulate my NYPD for the superlative job they did, and the FBI, who helped coordinate this operation. I'll take a few questions now."

He saw Breshill's hand shoot up. He called on him.

"Commissioner," Breshill said, "is this the end of the attack? Have all the players been caught now?"

Raymond weighed his words carefully. He didn't want to say anything that would alert Hamadi that they were onto him. "This is an ongoing investigation."

He was about to move to another question when Breshill continued to speak. "What about the grand jury? Why was DA Dannis not in charge of it?"

"We're here to discuss the tragic events of today. Next question, please," Raymond said. After taking two more, both directed to agent Jones, that were essentially reiterations of what had already been said, Raymond gave the podium back to the mayor, who ended the press conference by calling up the city's chaplain to say a prayer for the people of New York City and its brave police force and citizenry.

Back in his office, Raymond was filled in by Gallagher. Surveillance teams were out looking for Hamadi, and three teams were at the 41st Precinct waiting for him to show up. His phone had gone dead since the attack.

Raymond and Gallagher went over to FBI headquarters, and there they met with Jones. "We're thinking that Hamadi's car may have live explosives in it," she said. "We want to make sure he can't set them off when we take him. We have bomb techs standing by in the event that he shows up at the precinct for work, although we're not sure if he'll show. He may try to take off. His apartment is under surveillance, his girlfriend's house, and the mosque as well. We'll see."

No sooner than Jones finished the sentence, her cell phone rang and she answered it, hung up, smiled, and said, "It's on."

Hamadi had driven to the Bronx to report for his 11 pm tour of duty at the 41st Precinct, unaware that he had been made, and was looking to do nothing to draw attention to himself. "Let's go up to the Four-One," Jones said. "You jump in my car and your guys can follow us in the Suburban."

Raymond nodded to Gallagher, who called Archer to tell him they were moving. Sitting next to Jones in the back seat of the unmarked FBI vehicle, Raymond made a call on his cell phone. He speed-dialed Sammy Breshill's number, and the reporter picked up on the first ring. "What can I do for you, Commissioner?"

"Get your ass up to the 41st Precinct and wait down the block until I call you. Don't go inside; wait in your car. I think I've got something for you."

"Great."

"Yeah," Raymond said. "It is." He hung up.

He next called his chief of department, Joe Allegra, and told him to head to the Bronx as well, instructing him whom to look for and what to do with him when he got there. Allegra arrived ahead of the others, and when he walked into the Four-One, every cop—the desk sergeant, the desk lieutenant, and all 24 patrol officers present—snapped to attention. After a second or two, the desk officer resumed calling out who had what car and what the daily assignments were. When he finished, Allegra went up to the front desk.

The desk officer leaned over and forward to hear what Allegra had to say. "We're going to be doing a vest and weapons inspection. Everyone must be wearing a vest." The DO looked at Allegra for a second, searching for any clues about what was up, then ordered everyone present to line up in two rows, and open the top of his or her uniform shirt so he could see the bulletproof vest underneath.

Allegra then said, "Lieutenant John Picciano, from my office, who is standing on the side, is going to be checking your firearms. There was a cloud of confusion, but no one objected. One by one, the lieutenant took the automatic service weapon from each cop, walked over to the clearing barrel, cleared the weapon, checked the ammo, reloaded the gun, and walked back over to the officer and had him put it back in his holster.

Hamadi was in the second row of cops. The lieutenant took his weapon, went to the clearing barrel, pulled out the magazine, ejected the round in the chamber, reloaded the gun, but this time, instead of returning the gun, he stuck it into his own waistband. The other officers turned and looked at Hamadi. Just then, the commissioner,

Gallagher, and Jones and a number of FBI agents and police detectives walked through the door, with Breshill in tow, and just stood there.

Raymond whispered something in Allegra's ear and then turned to the front of the group. He stood at attention and then asked Hamadi to step front and center. He waited until Hamadi was there, directly in front of him. Raymond gave him a dead cold stare, leaned forward, and whispered into his ear, "You are a fucking piece of shit."

He took a step back and said, loud enough for everyone in the room to hear, "You are under arrest. Turn around and put your hands behind your back." Raymond looked at Allegra. "Cuff him."

Just then, Jones leaned over to Raymond and said, "We've got someone to do this." Raymond nodded. Allegra stepped back, and FBI special agent Michael Khoury, whom Raymond recognized from the FBI command center, walked directly in front of Hamadi.

With his long hair pulled back and tied into a ponytail, a full beard, and dark skin, there was no doubt he was of Middle Eastern descent. He Mirandized Hamadi, closed his cuffs around the officer's wrists, and said in Arabic, "You're a disgrace to every Muslim American, and every cop in this country." Hamadi said nothing as he stared at Khoury with murder in his eyes.

Breshill, still standing near the door, watched the arrest of Hamadi go down, then was shoved out of the way as nearly a dozen FBI agents and NYPD cops walked Hamadi out and placed him in a Bureau car. It then sped off in a six-car caravan to 26 Federal Plaza.

Raymond, Jones, and Breshill walked out the front door of the precinct in time to watch an NYPD robot close in on Hamadi's vehicle, while just outside the gate, bomb dogs were being held with tight leashes, ready to do their thing.

Breshill was out of his mind; Raymond had given him the whole thing, exclusive, and he had made notes of everything on his small spiral pad. Raymond turned to him and said, "Now do your job and report something that's worth reporting for once."

CHAPTER 12

7:30 am, Saturday, 14 October .

Raymond had gotten a much-needed full night's sleep, and was in his office by seven the next morning. In front of him was the early edition of the *New York Herald*. The headline read:

COMMISSIONER TAKES OUT TERROR COP

Story by Sammy Breshill starts on page 3

As Raymond read Breshill's story, impressed with its accuracy and attention to detail, he knew this was not the end of anything. He couldn't relax or bask in the capture of Hamadi. He knew the mastermind in Detroit was probably reading the same story, taking it all in. The way these cells worked, the cell members operated independently once they received their orders. No one knew who anyone else was, and each member only reported to one person, in this case, the guy in Detroit. Raymond knew he had to get him before the next attack took place. For all he knew, New York may have been a dry run, to see where the flaws were in the plan. Raymond was sure the next phase was likely already in place and ready to go.

His cell phone rang. It was Sheilah. He punched her in. "What are you doing tonight? You have time for dinner? How about that Italian spot in Jersey City?"

"I'll be there at eight," he said and hung up. The nondescript Italian restaurant in Jersey City was just on the other side of the Holland Tunnel. He then went across the street to meet up with the mayor, and together they held another press conference, one that was carried all over the world on CNN International. The eyes of the world on both sides of the war were on them.

That night, Shelby and Archer drove him to Jersey City in the unmarked black Suburban. When they arrived, Raymond got out and was escorted by Archer through the back door of the restaurant to the private dining room, where Sheilah was waiting for him. As the curtain closed behind them, they kissed. Sheilah reached down and felt his hardness. "My, my, Commissioner, you're always armed and ready!"

He wanted to laugh, but he didn't. Instead, they sat in their banquette, close, and shared martinis. "Tell me about your day, darling," she murmured. That did get a laugh from Raymond.

Archer left through the back, but did not go directly to the car. Instead, he surveyed the street from the shadow of the alley, stopping when he saw Breshill's car pull up. How the fuck did he know where we were, Archer wondered, as he called Gallagher on his cell.

"Okay," Gallagher said. "Leave the commissioner alone to finish, but let him know before he comes out."

Gallagher, too, wondered how Breshill could possibly have known where they were, and was annoyed that the tip they had given him about Hamadi apparently hadn't been enough. Okay, plan B, he told himself.

Archer waited until they finished dinner, then advised Raymond that Breshill was outside in his car. Raymond was pissed off. He told Sheilah to remain behind for about 15 minutes; then he and Archer walked out to his car and left.

Sheilah waited and then left the restaurant. Outside, her driver pulled the car up, and as she was about to get in, Breshill came up to her. He had dashed over as soon as he saw her. "Madame DA," he said, "I'd like to ask you about your personal relationship with the police commissioner." He had his pen and pad out. Sheilah stared at him, said nothing, and got into the back seat of her car. Her driver took off, leaving Breshill standing alone in front of the restaurant.

As soon as her car emerged on the Manhattan side of the tunnel, she punched in Raymond's number on her cell. He picked up immediately. He was, by now, almost home in Riverdale. Sheilah told him what happened. "We need to find out how this fucking guy knows every move we make," Raymond said, as his phone began to buzz. "I've got to take this," he said, and promised to call her back.

It was Jones. "Detroit is talking to two players, one right outside of Fort Bragg, North Carolina, the other in Vegas."

"Anything new from Hamadi?" Raymond asked.

"Negative. We have JTTF teams from New York and Detroit on the way to Fayetteville, and two of my guys are heading to Las Vegas to personally assist and supervise. We know this—whatever they're planning, it appears it's going to happen the same day, same time. We believe we have 10 days to stop it."

"Okay," Raymond said. "Keep me in the loop."

"Will do."

It was nearly midnight by the time he got back to his apartment. He opened the door, took his jacket off in the living room, walked into the bedroom where he dropped his clothes, and then went back to the living room and sat down on the couch. Taking some documents he had to go over, he spread them out on the glass coffee table. As he started to read, his mind drifted to Breshill, and within minutes, fell asleep on the couch, his pen still in his hand.

He was awakened at 4:30 in the morning by a call on his cell phone. It was Gallagher. "Two cops involved in a motor vehicle accident in Brooklyn . . . injuries serious, not critical, both stable."

"Okay," Raymond said, blinking himself awake. "I'll see them first thing in the morning, but listen, we need to find out how this fucking reporter knows my every move."

"I agree," Gallagher said, and Raymond hung up. He figured he could squeeze another hour of sleep in. He never bothered to get off the couch, just stretched out and slipped back into nightmare-land.

CHAPTER 13

8:15 am, Monday, 16 October

Gallagher arrived at his office at One Police Plaza, next to Raymond's, and while having his first cup of coffee, called in Bob Timmins, the captain in charge of the commissioner's protective detail. He gestured for Timmins to sit down in the chair opposite the desk.

"Okay," Gallagher said, "we have a problem. How does this reporter Breshill know every move the commissioner makes, on duty and off? Everywhere he goes. How is that even possible? I hate to say it, but is it possible this fucker has a tracking device on his car? How is it possible?! Could it be one of our guys?"

The captain stared back at Gallagher, wondering if he had lost his mind. "No way, sir. There's no way."

"All right," Gallagher said, raising his hands as if he were waving, "then he must have a device under our car. How else could he know everything?"

"We can try something," Timmins said. He picked up Gallagher's desk phone and punched in the number of the department's deputy commissioner of technology. While he was holding, he asked Gallagher to write down the reporter's cell phone number. "Listen," the captain said, when the deputy commissioner came on the line, "the commissioner wants you to run this number through our system. I need to know any cell phone or hard line department phone that calls that number."

"Roger."

"Today."

"Yes, sir." The deputy commissioner hung up the phone. "I'll let you know how we make out."

Gallagher nodded his head and gestured with his hand for Timmins to leave. As Timmins got to the door, Gallagher repeated, "Today."

"Roger that."

Raymond arrived at eight-thirty, poured himself a cup of black coffee, sat down at his desk, and checked his messages. The first slip had Gallagher's name on it. He walked over to the door to Gallagher's office, opened it, and said, "Come here." When Gallagher walked into the office, Raymond held up the pink slip. He was smiling as he said, "Why do you find it necessary to give Janey your messages to me, when your door is closer to mine than hers, and you have a direct intercom to me and can walk in here anytime you please? Yet you feel the need to leave a fucking message with Janey?"

Gallagher had a big shit-eating grin on his face while Raymond was on his rant, and when Raymond had concluded, Gallagher said, "Every once in a while I walk in here and you give a look like I'm intruding on your territory, so I figured I'd just give you some space and act like the rest of your minions and make an appointment."

"You're an asshole," Raymond said, laughing as he threw the crumpled-up pink slip at Gallagher. Then he asked, "What are we going to do about this fucking reporter?"

Gallagher was holding a container of coffee in one hand and a half-eaten roll in the other, crumbs spilling down the front of his shirt as he took a bite. He took a wash-down sip before speaking. "I'm on it. I've got Timmins checking something out. Give us a day or two." Raymond nodded his head up and down, frowned, and told Gallagher to keep him informed every step of the way as they both got up and went to the conference room for the morning cabinet meeting.

They were last to arrive. Already there were Department Chief Allegra, First Deputy Commissioner Joe Nagle, the other deputy commissioners, and all the bureau chiefs, ready to discuss the business of the day. First came a review of the city's crime numbers. They were down, which pleased Raymond. A city councilman's daughter was busted for possession. One of the mayor's assistants was involved in a domestic dispute. The deputy commissioner of budget and management reported that he was unable to come to terms with the mayor's budget office. "If they take any more money out of special ops, all of our horses in the mounted unit will die because there will be no hay to feed them."

Raymond listened to all of it, thinking to himself that he was working in a fucking insane asylum. "The horses won't die," he told the deputy commissioner.

The bureau chief of Internal Affairs wanted to discuss, in private, a corruption case involving a police sergeant. Raymond stared at him for a few seconds; then he said, "All of the top men and women in this department are sitting in this room, including the chief of department, the first deputy, the chief of patrol, and the chief of detectives, but you want to see me in private? Tell me who in this room you do not trust, and I'll ask them to leave, but I honestly believe it's okay to discuss a corruption case with everyone in this room listening, because if they're not to be trusted, they don't deserve to be here. Now, what do you have?"

His face red from the dress-down, the chief of Internal Affairs said, "We have a sergeant who's been taking money from the drug dealers for protection."

"Good," Raymond said. "Lock him up. Let's move on."

When everyone around the room had finished speaking, Raymond looked at Chief Allegra and said, "Listen, call the precinct commander up at the 19th Precinct. Let him know that I received a call from the mayor at 11:30 last night, and again at 6:30 this morning, complaining about panhandlers on 96th Street by the FDR Drive. If I get one more fucking call from the mayor, I'm going to stick a van on that corner, and that's where the precinct commander is going to have his new office. You got that?"

The chief looked at him and said, "I got it."

"Thanks, everyone," Raymond said, and got up and walked out.

Because of all the recent upheavals and killings, this was a day Raymond had designated to stay out of the public eye and catch up on some of his office work, while he continued to wait for the grand jury to hand down its decision.

He had forgotten how good it felt to sit behind a desk, take care of the day-to-day business, and plan a normal dinner with Sheilah, without killing anybody, or some mass chaos.

Precisely at 9:00 his phone began to ring, and kept ringing every 15 minutes. When he wasn't on the phone, he was taking meetings via conference calls. He worked that way, uninterrupted, through lunch. He had Archer call out for a turkey on whole wheat with lettuce, tomato, and mayo, and a diet Coke, and ate while reading the *Herald*, bypassing the cover story that had somehow gotten a photo of the minivan just at the moment it was blowing up. Later that afternoon, he was planning to head up to the Bronx for a town hall meeting with community leaders who had been complaining of rampant drug dealing in the streets.

At 2:30 pm, just as he was preparing to head uptown, his personal cell rang. It was Gallagher, who was in Chinatown having a dumpling lunch. "I know you're heading up to the Bronx shortly, but I'm on the way over, and I need to see you before you leave. I'm having the first dep head that way in case you're running late, but this is important."

"What?"

"I just got word on who's leaking to the reporter. Someone in your office is telling him every move you make," Gallagher said. "I'm on my way."

Gallagher arrived 20 minutes later. Raymond poured them each a cup of coffee, and they sat in the chairs in front of the desk. Gallagher began, "So we ran the reporter's cell through the department's technology bureau. Turns out that there's a number in the outer office, calls him 5 to 10 times a day, all day, all night."

Raymond frowned, "Who?"

"We narrowed it down to a block of phones in the protocol office, and we discovered that same number that calls the reporter is also calling Taylor Shelby the same amount of times, if not more."

"Shelby," Raymond said grimly, as if pronouncing sentence on a prisoner. "Are you sure? I just can't believe it. It just can't be."

"Maybe not him," Gallagher said. "There's a female in the protocol office—Mandy Walker—who's fucking around with Shelby. She may also be fucking Breshill. Every time after she talks to Shelby, she calls the reporter."

Raymond's eyebrows went up in a mixture of genuine surprise and amusement. "That little twerp Breshill gets laid?"

Gallagher continued, "I already spoke to Shelby. He admitted to me he's been seeing this chick for six months and that they talk several times a day. Whenever he's driving the Suburban and waiting for you, he calls her to bullshit, and he'll tell her where he is or what he's up to. He swears he never gives up anything personal about you; just figured she was part of the team and never thought twice about saying where he was at any given time. He had no idea he was giving away secrets, and that they were going straight to Breshill. He also didn't know she was fucking both of them. He's more devastated over that than just being a jerk."

"He should be," Raymond said, suppressing a smile.

"We haven't approached her yet. You're going to leave the office in a little while, to go up to the Bronx, and Taylor will tell her where you are. He's going to make it sound hot and juicy, and if that fucking reporter shows up, we'll know for sure it's her."

Raymond looked at Gallagher for a long time, and finally put his coffee cup down on the edge of the desk. "Is she married?" he asked Gallagher.

"Yes. All three of them are. I think of it as some kind of mass cluster mind-fuck."

Now they both started laughing, until the phone rang. Janey told him it was FBI agent Jones. "I've got to take this," Raymond said to Gallagher. He cleared his throat to make sure he sounded serious.

"Chelsea?"

"Rick. Looks like whatever they're planning is going down Friday next week. They're still working on trying to ID the talkers and their exact locations."

"Good work," Raymond said.

Jones continued, "Our guys in Vegas and North Carolina are infiltrating all the local mosques, collecting as much intel as they can. Hopefully, we'll locate those actors before they can hit."

"Terrific." Then Raymond paused and said, "Jones, what are you doing for dinner? Any plans?"

"I was thinking maybe a Shake Shack and after a couple of beers."

"I know a nice little place on the Upper East Side. Let's meet there and try to make a plan, say 7:30?"

"Good."

"Hold on. My assistant will give you the address." Raymond hung up and told Janey to give Shelby the evening schedule. "Let's see what happens."

At 8:15 pm, Shelby, Archer, and Gallagher were sitting in the Suburban outside the restaurant, when Gallagher saw Breshill in his side-view mirror, on foot, turning the corner and walking toward the restaurant. Gallagher called Raymond, who was already inside the restaurant with Jones; then he got out of the car and approached Breshill. Raymond excused himself and walked outside, where Breshill, who was never surprised by anything, look genuinely caught off guard. The reporter was standing with Gallagher, looking openly scared, even more so when Raymond came into his view.

"Sam," Raymond said, walking right up to Breshill and putting his face in the reporter's, "Your scam's over, and your girlfriend's fucked. How would you like it if I called your wife and told her you're fucking one of my detectives? I hope you make enough to support the three of you, because I'm going to fire your babe's ass tomorrow morning before coffee. And if your wife doesn't know, she's going to." He stared at Breshill for several elongated seconds, and then turned around and walked away and left Breshill standing there next to Gallagher, who had a silly smirk on his face.

Breshill stood there looking at Gallagher as if he were waiting for permission to leave, and Gallagher said, "Listen, you fucked up. You don't like the mayor, so you've haunted this guy for a fucking year now over bullshit. It's wrong and you know it."

"What's he going to do?" Breshill asked, looking as if he were being sent to the gas chamber.

"Who knows, but I wouldn't want to be your girlfriend or your wife unless you figure out a way to make it right." With that, Gallagher walked to the Suburban, got in, and closed the door, leaving Breshill standing there.

CHAPTER 14

10:30 pm, Monday, 16 October

Sheilah was a little punchy by the time Raymond arrived at the Marcus penthouse. She had come from a fund-raiser for the governor, one of the few events she didn't mind going to because she needed that network in the future, if and when she ran for mayor the next time around. But all the glad-handing was tiresome and she was anxious to get back to something real.

In addition to his powerful personality, she also appreciated that Raymond was a good-looking man. His six-foot, two-inch muscularly sculpted frame made it obvious that even with his 16-hour-a-day job, he still made time for the gym. Had they not held the jobs they did and had they made their relationship public, they could have been the best-looking and most powerful couple in the state of New York. Rick had the perfect combination of good looks, street smarts, and from-the-gut appeal, and Sheilah had smarts and telegenic charisma; they had real-life command.

She stared into the bathroom mirror as she began the intricate process of bringing her face back to normal, rather than the pan-caked, eyelashed, eyelinered, blow-dried, lipsticked professional offi-cial the public saw. She always began by peeling off the thick black fake eyelashes, slowly and carefully so as not to make her eyelids swell. She studied herself in the mirror as if she were performing surgery, and Rick came in, as always, sat on the closed toilet seat, to observe, sometimes with wonder, the intricate operation. She liked it when he watched her take her face off, knowing how much he appreciated her natural beauty. It became something erotic to the both of them.

After only a few minutes, Rick stood, went behind her, and unzipped her stiff ball gown, as she moved her face closer to the mir-ror. That close, she could only see the side of Rick's head. His silvery sideburns, she thought to herself, made him look so distinguished. Most men would kill to have a full head of hair like his. He combed it, blow-dried it, styled it with any one of a number of products he kept on his sink. He preened sometimes, which to her was a sign of his vanity, which normally she would consider a sign of weakness, but she thought Raymond contradicted her theory, because he was definitely all man, from head to toe. The way he . . .

"Darling?" Rick interrupted her dream-thought. "Drop your hands and let your dress fall to the floor. I'll hang it up." She did so, and it fell. Rick stared at her back for a second, marveling as he always did at the dimpled muscles just below her shoulders. All those years of tennis showed her off well, and the two dimples just above her athletic backside.

Rick slipped his hand around her waist, pulling her aggressively into him (just the way she liked). She shrugged and wiggled at the same time, until she was free of his grip, teasing him. "Rick," she said, matter-of-factly, "I'm trying to take off my face."

He stood up behind her. "You don't like it?" Smiling, looking at her in the mirror.

"Please, darling . . ."

He let go of her waist, massaged her back, helping her release the tensions of the day.

She stopped, turned around, and looked down to face him, then leaned over, putting her face up close to his, sticking out her tongue and licking his lips. "You need to behave yourself, for just a few minutes, and I'll reward you for your good behavior, but I cannot with your octopus hands all over me. Go get in the bed, and I will be there shortly."

Like an obedient child, Raymond got up and walked into the bedroom, pulled down the rich bedding, and crawled under. Within 30 seconds, he was dozing off, thinking about Breshill, and feeling relieved that he now had closed that leak in the department.

A few minutes later Sheilah came into the bedroom of the suite, wearing her silk beige robe, the one that came to just above her knees. "Darling," she said, as she slid in besides him and kissed his cheek to wake him up. "What's on your mind? You seemed a little distant tonight."

"No, actually I'm not. Not at all," as he rolled over, kissed her. She loved being his pet. As powerful and aggressive as she was in her job, there was a place where she felt safe and secure, and that was in his arms, where she knew she'd always be protected, so she thought.

She could not imagine a time that her best friend, her protector, and the love of her life, wouldn't be there when she needed him.

Rick was in his office the next day by 6:30 am. The night before, Janie had his schedule for the day waiting for him on his desk. Two morning meetings, lunch with the mayor, a press conference, a stop-by at the academy, afternoon meeting with Fox News, 5:00 cocktails at City Hall for a subway something ceremony, dinner with the DA. He sat back, closed his eyes, and found himself a few hours forward in time to when he would see Sheilah in high heels, her pursed lips leaving a red imprint on her martini glass, the suite at the

Marcus smelling like fresh lilacs, her . . . He was yanked out of his daydream as Gallagher burst into the office, like he was on a SWAT team.

"What?" Raymond said, as Gallagher looked like he was on a mission.

"I'm going to talk to the girl—Mandy Walker— now. You want to come?"

"Leave me out of it. Get rid of her, but don't be too hard. Move her somewhere else; don't fire her. Let's keep her where we can have eyes on where she is and what she does. She still has Breshill's number. I think we got him neutralized, but let's make certain."

"Okay, I'll take care of it."

Gallagher went out past Janey, over to Mandy's desk. She was attractive, he thought to himself, too good for Breshill. For Shelby too. "Mandy, see you a minute? The second office is free."

"Sure," she said, bright as a light. She grabbed a note pad and her iPad as she stood. He was about to tell her she didn't need any of that, but he decided to let her think she did, and she followed him into the empty office.

"Sit down," Gallagher said. She took a seat, crossing her legs. "How's everything going, Mandy?"

"Fine," she said, a sincere smile on her face.

Gallagher parked himself on the side of the desk, so he was higher than she was, making her have to look up as he spoke, in his quiet, measured tones. "So here's the deal, Mandy. We don't want you to lose your job, or fuck up your marriage." He saw the smile start to droop and her jaw tighten.

"We're going to have to transfer you out of the office, so let me know by four o'clock today where you want to go."

Her eyes teared up. "What have I done? I didn't do anything!"

"Doesn't make a difference; you've got to go."

She put her face in her hands and started crying. "What did I do?" she managed to get out from behind her fingers.

"We know about your relationship with Breshill; we also know you have been feeding confidential information about the PC's movement, and although it's not a crime, you could be brought up on charges."

She looked up and stared at him. "I didn't . . ."

"Stop. You did. Maybe Breshill worked you, I don't know, and I don't care, but it ends here. Have your decision on my desk by four. It's the only way. Understand?"

She wiped the tears from her cheeks with her fingers and shook her head up and down quickly.

"Okay. Go wash your face."

He watched her leave. Too bad, he thought to himself.

He leaned out the door and told Archer to get Shelby, in the car, and tell him to come in.

When Shelby entered the room, he looked like he was about to be sent to the guillotine. Gallagher took him into that same room and proceeded to rip him a new asshole. Shelby started babbling and explaining that it was just BS conversation and she was a part of the office, so he didn't think anything of it when he told her things, never believing she was talking to a reporter.

Gallagher said, "You're lucky the boss loves you, but if it ever happens again, he'll have you walking a foot post in Alaska. Got it?"

"Yes sir."

"Now get the fuck out of here and go back to work. And keep your fucking mouth zipped." Back in his office, Gallagher called Breshill, who was downstairs in the press shack, the press office at NYPD headquarters all the reporters worked out of, and told him Raymond wanted to see him.

"When?" Breshill said, curious after his last encounter.

"Yesterday . . . Now, like right now."

"On my way."

When Breshill arrived, Gallagher met him at the elevator and brought him into Raymond's office himself, then stood off to the side and watched and listened.

"Sit down," Raymond said in a tone that could not be refused.

Raymond got up and went to the window, looked out for a few seconds, then came back to his desk and sat down opposite Breshill. "Look," Raymond said, "you don't like the mayor, so you don't like me, and yes I don't like you. I try to avoid the press; you want to make headlines. That makes us natural enemies, right? It doesn't have to be, but you've done everything you could to make it that way." He leaned over, closer to Breshill, as if to emphasize what he was about to say. "You used this Mandy girl; maybe she didn't know what you were doing, but you did. So, here's what we're going to do, from this point forward. You stay out of my personal life, and I'll stay out of yours. Understood?"

Breshill nodded.

"Good." Raymond then stuck out his hand to shake Breshill's hand, and just for a second, Breshill hesitated before he shook. "Let's have a drink sometime, and, you know what? I may have something for you in the future."

Breshill perked up. "Sure. A drink. Great." Then he smiled, nodded to Gallagher, left the office, and sped toward the elevator.

Gallagher looked at Raymond and said, "I thought you were going to kill him."

"For what, getting laid and doing his job? He's been neutralized, and, besides, we need as many friends at the *Herald* as we can get.

You learn something new every day, Gallagher said to himself.

CHAPTER 15

12:00 pm, Tuesday, 17 October

Raymond and Gallagher were about to leave when the desk phone buzzed. Raymond held up a hand to Gallagher and picked up the phone. "Janey?"

"Agent Jones is stopping over in 15."

"Fuck!" He hung up and looked at Gallagher. "Now what?"

Gallagher shrugged.

Twenty minutes later, Janey opened the door and Jones walked in. She shook hands with the two, then sat down on the sofa, while Gallagher moved toward the window, where he stood silently.

"Gentlemen," Jones began, "we discovered some encrypted files on one of Hamadi's hard drives. It took several unsuccessful tries but we were able to break it.

Usually, we can't crack them. That's the official Bureau line, what we want the enemy to think. Actually, we crack most of their chatter and code fairly quickly, in a matter of days."

Raymond said, "Everything here is on high alert, and there's a visible presence at all the surface and tunnel entrances and exits to the city, the Port Authority Bus Terminal, Penn Station, Grand Central Terminal, the Seaport . . ."

Jones interrupted him. "We don't think they are planning on hitting this city again."

"Then where?"

"We think it's going to be Las Vegas and Fayetteville, North Carolina. Anywhere in those areas it's legal to possess machine guns and other heavy weaponry. They probably think nobody will notice weapons movement there."

"More fucking nuts," Raymond said.

"Bad news," Jones said.

"If this guy did the two cops, and now this, we've got to take him out," Gallagher said.

Jones: "We've picked up chatter that makes us fairly certain they're going to hit two targets simultaneously. Keep in mind that Fort Bragg is in Fayetteville, the home of the Airborne Rangers, the 82nd Airborne, several Special Forces groups, and the John F. Kennedy Unconventional Warfare Center. It's perfect for them."

Raymond frowned. "Could they be that crazy?

"Yes," Jones said, "but there's a five-mile pedestrian walk just outside Fort Bragg—Bragg Boulevard. It goes from Hay Street all the way up to the entrance near the base, and it's filled with strip clubs, restaurants, and malls and shopping centers that service the soldiers. On any given day, there are thousands of GIs that hit these spots up and down that strip, not to mention their families. It's especially busy on Friday and Saturday nights; the strip clubs make the area a target-rich environment. These assholes love all the Western depravity they pretend they hate. It makes them look good to their people, but we know how much they love pornography, and they rape their own women as regularly as the queen takes tea."

"Same thing with Vegas," Raymond said. "It's the sex and sin capital of the country. The casinos are packed on weekends."

Jones stood up. "We're focused primarily on the base, but these guys could show up anywhere."

Late that evening, at the Marcus, Raymond and Sheilah were sitting up in bed, finishing off the last of a bottle of Laurent-Perrier. Sheilah was wearing a sheer, flowing beige silk robe, the robe falling open when she sat against the pillows with her knees up and bent. Raymond was back in his jockeys. "You seem distracted, Rick," she said, as she sipped the last of the champagne from her glass.

"Sorry."

"Breshill?"

Rick laughed and waved his hand. "He won't be bothering us anymore."

"Did you see the headline this morning?" She had the paper folded on the night table and held it up to show him the front page.

"I saw it," he said.

The front page screamed

DELIGHTFUL DA TO RUN FOR MAYOR?

Story by Sammy Breshill starts on page 3

"Well," Rick said, "It happens to be true."

"I still don't like it," Sheilah said, throwing the paper off the bed. She laid back, sinking deeper into her pillow, put her glass on the night table next to her. "Delightful . . . they wouldn't say that about a man! It's a sexist thing to say. It makes fun of and diminishes my abilities and my ambitions."

"He's a journalist, Sheilah. We can't stop him from doing his job." Rick took a last sip of his champagne. "At least he didn't call you Cruella de Vil."

"He better not if he wants to live."

A few minutes of silence passed. "What is it?" she finally said to him. "What's wrong?"

He took a deep breath, then spoke. "The FBI came by my office today. They think another attack is coming."

"In New York?"

"They don't think so, but I can't really get into it."

"Be careful." She took his drained glass and put it next to hers. "Lie back, warrior. You're too tense. Let me attack you, and I guarantee you, I won't stop until you surrender yourself to me."

Rick smiled. He had to admit, she had a way with words.

CHAPTER 16

2:30 am, Wedesday, 18 October

Rick left the Marcus and got home to Riverdale just before midnight. He hated leaving Sheilah, but needed to get fresh clothes and sometimes just needed some private time, to get his "off-duty" work done—his reading, writing, and transfer considerations. He removed his jacket, threw it on the sofa, and headed for the bathroom to get cleaned up and ready for bed. He was exhausted, from the day and from Sheilah, and hoped he could get in a few hours of sleep before going downtown. He smiled to himself. Sheilah must have really been pissed off at that headline; she'd given him an extra-rough going over.

He heard his cell phone buzz in his jacket pocket. He reached over the back of the sofa and pulled it out. Jones. He clicked her on.

"They hit. We were off on the date, or they intentionally threw us off."

"How bad?" Rick turned on the small kitchen TV and turned on CNN with the sound off. He could see all hell breaking loose.

"Bad. There's more."

"Hit me."

"Vegas and NC. Just before the shooter shot up a strip club near Fort Bragg, he called Samadi to say goodbye, and then said, 'Is for carriers of God that we will visit Lady Liberty.' We think he has four guys already in the city."

"Meet me at our operations center. I'll have someone waiting for you. I'll be there in 30 minutes."

"There's something else."

"It can wait. Let's move." He speed-dialed Gallagher. "Tell the guys to get my car ready and pick me up in 20 minutes, and get hold of the first dep and chief. Have them start to secure all the cities' soft targets, religious sites, government buildings, tourist locations, and anything else they can think of. Activate our Emergency Operations Center and monitor everything that went down in North Carolina and Vegas. And keep everything under wraps. We don't want to set off a panic and tip these bastards that we're on to them."

"That it?"

"We are not going to let them hit this city again."

"Got it," Gallagher said.

"Let's go."

The Pink Pussy Dance Club is situated midway along Bragg Boulevard. It had a reputation among the soldiers as the place with the youngest and prettiest, and hottest, dancers, some pretty local girls, but the hottest ones were imported from other cities, playing a circuit that took them to all the best stops. The entrance to the Pink Pussy, as the soldiers called it, was from the rear, through the main parking lot, where it cost $10 to park and $20 to get your wrist stamped, a different color "V" with a new tail every night, to prevent freebies.

It was almost midnight, and, as always at the witching hour, the place was packed. Electrobeat was pounding from the 35 Bose 902s hung from the ceiling, while red lights swirled around the room, making it look like an overheated landing strip, or a prison break. Lollie, one of the headliners, was in the midst of her show. She had taken her top off by now and was about to slip out of her panties. The room had gotten noticeably quieter, as the young recruits studied her body like they were in the theater of a medical school. Lollie was in the middle of the stage, on her back, her legs straight up in the air, her thumbs hooked into the top of her panties, as she slowly wriggled them off. Dollar bills were being tossed at her like dice at a craps table, and the ice-cold bottles of beers were being drunk by the dozen.

No one noticed the young, average looking, swarthy man walk in, or the weapon strapped to the inside of his pants leg. Once inside the entrance doors, he reached down, pulled up the Kalashnikov, and opened fire. He hit the hefty black bouncers first, who were nearest to him and unarmed. They fell like bowling pins as they were cut in half by the force of the shooter's weapon. As everybody turned toward the entrance, the shooter began mowing down soldiers. Bodies fell as he moved his weapon in a semicircle, back and forth. Lollie never knew what hit her, and it was hard to see how much of her blood spread across the stage floor because of those red lights.

Screams pierced the air as the music abruptly stopped and the house lights came up. Bodies continued to fall, making it even more difficult for those still alive to get to the front exits. There was pushing and shoving, and bodies continued to fall.

The shooter suddenly stopped firing and fell in a single motion as his gun went up in the air, flying out of his hands, floating for a few seconds like a loaded missile. A Cumberland County sheriff's deputy had slipped in the back door, raised his Glock, put it on the back of the shooter's head, and blew his brains out. His eyes and nose flew off the front of his face, and bits of his shattered teeth flew out of his mouth. He was dead before he hit the ground, never even having a chance to say *Allahu Akbar*. He'd have to get to those 72 virgins without saying please or thanks.

Dozens of Fayetteville police joined the deputy sheriff as they flooded into the nightclub, along with several U.S. Army MP investigators and federal agents, who tried to move out the survivors through the emergency exit door and make a path for the medics to get in. Ambulances began arriving, sirens screaming. The first body count was 12, but before the medics were finished, it had tripled, as bodies were moved and revealed more dead underneath.

Across the country, in Las Vegas, it was a blistering night. The temperature had reached 110 degrees during the day, and it was still in the 90s as midnight approached. The Prospect Hotel was filled that weekend with young people, because Katy Kelly had performed earlier that night. The young girls were all tanned from hanging out at the pool, and the boys were wearing their best clubbing muscle outfits. Vegas was the easiest place in the West to score. Girls came there to get laid, and boys were all too willing to accommodate them, and nobody brought anything home with them.

When the show had ended at 9:30, the audience packed into the already full casino. Money was flowing, and so were the drinks, when the shooter came in. This was Vegas, and all anybody cared about was the money. Customers wanted to spend it; security wanted to make sure nobody left with what wasn't theirs. In this desert town, everybody was welcome at every casino. Security was not obtrusive, but just outside the floor of the casino, in the stations concealed from the public, SWAT teams were at the ready. The shooter never made it through his first magazine. He was spotted on a monitor pulling up his weapon, and the team came out firing. The shooter managed to take five out—two female guests, two male, and a dealer—before they brought him down. As he fell, he detonated an explosive vest strapped to his body, and the entire casino exploded. Everything and everyone within 30 feet of the bomber shattered into bits and pieces as they funneled up in the death cloud. Ambulances arrived, and local cops and FBI pushed through the smoke, the flames, and the falling debris, weapons drawn, looking for survivors.

It was the second massacre of the night. Same day, same time, 2,031 miles apart.

Raymond rushed to 26 Federal Plaza. Jones was already there waiting for him in front of the building, and together the three of them, Jones, Raymond, and Gallagher, went up to the FBI's operations center, while Archer and Shelby stayed downstairs in the Suburban. All the while, Jones's cell phone had not stopped ringing, and when she got to her desk, she could see the landlines lit up. She told one of the agents to get to her assistant's desk and field the calls.

"What's it look like?" Raymond asked Jones.

Jones told him to sit down. "41 total, so far; 36 in NC and at least 5 in Vegas. The numbers will go higher in Vegas, for sure," she said. She paused to answer the ringing of her cell phone, and 30 seconds into the call, she began asking the person on the other end, "Are you sure?" Her eyes were locked onto Raymond's the whole time.

She appeared to get teary-eyed, cupped the phone, and excused herself, leaving Raymond sitting there alone. "Are you certain that it is him," he heard her ask again as she disappeared into the next room. Three minutes later, she returned and looked straight at Raymond, her face twisted and wet. "Rick, I've got something I have to tell you," she said. "We were hitting houses in NC and Vegas, searching for accomplices."

"Good," Raymond said.

Jones hesitated before continuing. "We just hit a house in NC. Two agents were killed, as well as one of your detectives."

"My God," Raymond said. "My nephew, Jimmy, he's . . . he's working with you guys in Fayetteville."

"He's dead," Jones said, her voice flat and sad.

Raymond's eyes widened; his mouth opened in shock. When he could speak again, he said, "Are you sure?"

"I'm sure, Rick. I'm so sorry."

Raymond hung his head, covered his face with his hands, and wept, as Jones sat across from him and watched. Through his fingers, he said, "How am I going to tell my sister Linda?" More weeping. "I loved Jimmy. I took care of him after his father died . . . I made sure he got the best gig down there . . . he was so happy, so much to look forward to . . ."

"I'm sorry," Jones said again. "He was part of the local police team that was with us hitting houses. One was booby-trapped, and as soon as they entered, all three, two agents and Jimmy, were killed instantly."

"Samadi," Raymond said slowly, as he took his hands away and stared at Jones, who could see murder in the commissioner's eyes.

Tom Thomas, the NYPD's deputy commissioner of public information, called Gallagher's cell. "The phones are going fucking crazy," he said. "CBS has suspended regular broadcasting, and they want to know if you can . . ."

Gallagher stopped him. "Jimmy, the PC's nephew at JTTF was killed down in North Carolina."

"Jesus, no," Thomas said. "How?"

"They were hitting a house that was booby-trapped."

"Oh my God. Does the boss know yet?"

"Yes. I'm over at 26 Fed Plaza with him. He just found out."

Raymond walked out of Jones's office in a daze, followed by Jones and Gallagher, who called Archer and told him they were coming out, that Jimmy had been killed and they were heading to the commissioner's sister Linda's house in Queens. Gallagher then called Chief Allegra and First Deputy Nagle and told them about Jimmy; he ordered them to get ahold of the ceremonial unit and the chaplain's office and have the chief chaplain meet them at Linda's house, and also call the department CARE unit that takes care of the families of members of the service killed in the line of duty.

Raymond got into the back of the Suburban, with Gallagher next to him.

He looked at Jones, who was standing outside the SUV. "I'll call you later. I want to get his body back here as soon as possible."

"Call me when you can," Jones said. "I'll work on the logistics now; just go do what you've got to do."

"Thanks. We'll talk," he said. Then he looked at Archer and said, "Get to my sister Linda's house ASAP. I can't let her hear from anyone else first."

"I've got the chaplain meeting us there," Gallagher said.

"Tell him to wait for us to get there, before he goes to the door," Raymond said, then lowered his head. "Please God, don't let her find out from someone else," he said again, this time in a low voice. He looked at his watch; it was 4:45 am, and he had not slept yet. "Jerry, get the mayor's guys to call me the second he wakes up."

"You should call him now. He'd want to know this."

"You're right; dial his cell." Gallagher did, then handed Raymond the phone.

The mayor looked at the clock and saw the time and then answered the phone: "Hello. Everything okay?" Raymond went to speak, but nothing came out. It was like something knocked the breath out of him. The mayor said, "Are you okay?"

"Jimmy, my nephew, Linda's son, is dead." Crying almost uncontrollably, "They killed my nephew."

CHAPTER 17

6:00 am, Wednesday, 18 October

They arrived at Linda's house just after six in the morning. About six vehicles in total, but Raymond ordered them not to approach the house until the lights came on and they knew his sister was awake. At 6:45 am, the front hall light went on and then the kitchen light. Raymond, the chaplain, and a few uniformed chiefs approached the front door. Linda was in her robe when she answered the door, and at the sight of the chaplain, collapsed. She was hysterical in the living room, and when Raymond went to hold her, she pounded his chest with her fists, "How could you let him become a cop," she screamed, before her eyes rolled back and she collapsed again on the floor.

As the group tried to console her, the entire block outside her house filled up with marked and unmarked police cars as friends, colleagues, and cops assigned to assist the family began to arrive. Soon enough, the house inside and out was like a fortress, completely taken over by members of the department and a few FBI agents that Jimmy worked with. In the middle of all this commotion, Raymond's cell phone starting ringing. He looked down at it. Sheilah. He quietly excused himself, explaining it was police headquarters, and walked out the heavy front door of Linda's home to take it.

"Rick," Sheilah said. "I'm so sorry. So, so sorry."

"Thanks," he said, not knowing what else to say.

"Jones called and told me. That poor boy." She paused. "Can I see you later?"

"I'll call you later today. Right now I have to deal with Linda. She's a mess."

"I want to hold you. Now."

"I know," he said. "I gotta go." He ended the call and walked back into the house. He was met by the dead stare of Linda, who was surrounded by about 100 cops looking at him, wishing that he could make it all go away. He walked over to her, got on his knees, placed his hands in hers in her lap, and whispered, "Listen to me. Jimmy was the best of the best. That's why he was in the unit. That's exactly where he wanted to be and what he wanted to be doing. He died living his lifelong dream. Remember when he was a little boy . . . at six years old he wanted to be a cop, and he never wavered. He lived out his dream, and died doing exactly what he wanted." She leaned into him, their heads touching, as she sobbed quietly. He kissed her on the cheek, and then he said he was sorry he had to go downtown and he would call as soon as he could. Outside, as he got into the car, he said to Archer, "Let's get to headquarters. Tell the chief and first dep we're on the way, and to meet us there."

There was chaos inside Police Plaza. A bank of microphones was up live in the big room, and Raymond and the mayor were scheduled for a 9 am joint press conference. In his office, Raymond sipped his second cup of coffee and told Janey to hold his calls. He leaned back in his chair and went over in his mind what had happened after he'd gotten home.

His phone was lit up like the Rockefeller Center tree at Christmas. He took a few calls from reporters—those he liked—and answered all their questions and accepted their sympathies.

Then there was Jones. "I'm going to North Carolina for the bodies. Do you want to come with me? You can claim Jimmy's body and bring it back for burial."

"Yes. When?"

"I'm on the way to you, for the press conference. Right after, we'll head to the airport. The Bureau is sending a jet. See you in a few."

They took off from LaGuardia at 11 am and were on the ground in Fayetteville by 12:15. As they deplaned, a gentle southern breeze caressed Raymond's face. At the bottom of the ramp, dozens of FBI agents and local cops escorted them to a private area of Regional/ Grannis Field Airport reserved for military personnel and FBI operations. There, an agent and a U.S. Army captain from the 18th Airborne Corps stationed at Fort Bragg escorted them to an enormous refrigerator in the private area where coffins were stored. Both Jones and Raymond declined to have any of them opened for inspection. Raymond did not want to see Jimmy this way, and he would not let anyone else. Jones then took Raymond to a private dining room to have coffee, and, if he wanted, a bite to eat, while the coffins were loaded onto several planes, to be dispersed at various hubs, according to where the military and male and female agents were from. Jimmy's would be going back on the same plane Raymond and Jones came down on and would return to New York City in.

They found a table in the back, Jones put her bag down, and a server came over to ask what they wanted. They ordered two coffees, black, no food. She nodded and left.

Jones spoke first. "Rick, so sorry for you and your family."

"Thanks," Raymond said as the coffee came.

He stirred his with the stick, added nothing, instead taking a sip. It was scalding. "Military hot," Jones said.

"I want the people behind this . . . I need to have that."

"I know . . . we'll get them, but it's got to be done and done right. We'll get them."

Raymond looked at her and thought to himself, not the way I'd like to.

"Will there be anything else?" the waitress said.

"No," Jones said. Then she turned to Rick. "Let's go. The planes are probably loaded by now."

Raymond was back in his office by four that afternoon, greeted by a pile of messages stacked like an unruly deck of cards. He flipped through them, saw the mayor's name, and had Janey call him back.

Janey buzzed when she had him on the phone, Raymond picked up. "Mayor."

"Rick. Sorry about all of this."

"Thanks."

"Cardinal Dean called. He wants to know if you want Jimmy's funeral at St. Patrick's."

"Yes, but I need to check with Linda about when. I would imagine it should be Monday. Tell Cardinal Dean thanks from the family. Once I get word from Linda, I'll have the ceremonial unit start making arrangements."

"Are you doing okay?" the mayor asked.

"Yeah." Raymond paused, took a breath, and continued, "I just want the fuckers that did this. They've killed two of ours in the past month. I want them, and I want them dead."

"I'm sure . . . Let's get through this first. If you, Linda, or anyone in the family needs anything, or any help with the arrangements for the funeral, don't hesitate to call me."

"Thanks," Raymond said and hung up the phone. He stared out the window from his desk seat, his lips twitching as he wiped the sweat from his brow. "I want them dead," he repeated out loud, to nobody but himself.

That Friday night around eight, Raymond met Sheilah at the Marcus. After a quick drink at the bar, they headed up to her suite and stayed there for the entire weekend. Raymond poured his heart out to her, as if she were his own personal shrink. He talked about losing his wife, Mary, on 9/11 and how that day had changed him. He talked about Jimmy as a child, and how, since he had no kids of his own, he always treated Jimmy as if he were his. Sheilah tried to comfort him as much as she could, but it was obvious that he was dealing with his own personal demons; what was also clear to both of them was that the bond between them was stronger than ever and that they loved each other deeply. Saturday, after a room service breakfast, Sheilah tried to bring him around, using champagne as the fuel poured into her chassis, but there was something wrong with his starter. They spent the rest of the afternoon watching CNN with the sound off, dozing, cuddling, and caressing.

Sunday, he spent most of the day sleeping across her. This was the most rest he had gotten in the past month, and Gallagher and the team knew he needed it and left him alone. A few emergencies had come up, but Gallagher passed them off to Chief Allegra and First Deputy Commissioner Nagle, and told them that unless there was something earth-shattering, the PC was not to be called. Gallagher had worked for him for close to 10 years in different positions and had become accustomed to his work ethic. Three to five hours sleep daily for two to three months, and then one weekend, he'd do nothing but sleep and relax, but on that following Monday, he was like a hungry bear coming out from his annual hibernation. Deadly.

CHAPTER 18

9:00 am, Monday, 23 October

A light and warm drizzle washed down on Manhattan as thousands of police and mourners filled the streets of Fifth Avenue. All the way north to Central Park and south as far as 46th Street, police formations marched inside the barriers that had been placed along the sidewalks as a further layer of protection in the event of a terrorist attack. Behind them, thousands of pedestrians stood, some with umbrellas, most bareheaded, to mourn the loss of Jimmy Kerrigan, a local boy no one had ever heard of until he was killed in Fayetteville. He became, to them, every victim who had died at the hands of terrorists, and one of their own, the nephew of the city's police commissioner. How many times had they turned to him in the past, whenever the city had been under siege from terrorists, or experienced natural catastrophes? Now, they wanted to show their support, their love, for him and the city in which they all lived. Nothing, least of all a little rain, would keep them away.

Inside St. Patrick's, white wreaths tied with black bows hung from the columns, and chrysanthemums graced the altar, behind Jimmy's closed mahogany casket that was covered by the green, blue, and white flag of the NYPD. To the right of the casket, a giant photo of a smiling Jimmy in full-dress police uniform sat on a large brass easel, draped with a black ribbon. TV cameras were discreetly placed in platforms around the grand arena of the storied Catholic house of worship. The service was being broadcast nationwide, and picked up, via satellite, all around the world, for anyone who wanted to see it. In a remarkably short amount of time, the double attack had become a symbol of all victims of terror, and of the determination of Americans to defeat Islamic fundamentalist terrorism.

Raymond was seated in the first row of pews, on the right, with Linda and her estranged second husband, Kelly, and their younger son, Tommy, sitting next to him. Raymond felt a wave of regret wash over him, wishing that he had never assigned Jimmy to JTTF, lamenting that he didn't protect him in some way. To his left were the mayor and his wife, the governor and his wife, and Sheilah Dannis; then Jones and then Gallagher. The second row, on both sides, was filled with FBI agents and NYPD security personnel with weapons hidden from view. After that, filling in the rest of the pews, Jimmy's friends and other relatives, his unit, and anyone from the public able to get through the triple screening at the front doors, that, because it was an unusually warm fall day, were left open and guarded. From outside, the sound of bagpipes blowing "Amazing Grace" drifted through the open doors, as their procession marched on Fifth Avenue, headed south, until their mournful sound slowly faded away. St. Patrick's enormous pipe organ then filled the church with its grand, ringing sound that signaled the formal beginning of the funeral ceremonies.

After the Latin prayers were completed, St. Pat's Cardinal Dean went to the raised podium, off to the left of the coffin, his lectern lit with white spots hung high from the ceiling grid. "Ladies and gentlemen," he said in a lowered voice, his cheeks, as always, rosy and flushed, his robes shiny and reflective of the hundreds of candles lit throughout the cathedral. And as he began to speak, the low murmur throughout the church gave way to an unspoken hush. "Young Jimmy Kerrigan was blessed with many things, except, perhaps, the gift of long life. Now, he has been greeted into heaven by the Good Lord, where he will be taken into the family of good men. Jimmy looks down on us today, and we will always be able to look up and feel his spirit within us." The cardinal paused, looked over the congregated faces, then continued. "As a member of our great New York City police force, young Jimmy gave his life in the service of his country . . ."

As the cardinal continued, Raymond looked over to Linda, whose eyes remained focused on the service. He stared at her for several seconds, but she never turned his way. He then looked the other way, to where Sheilah was sitting, dressed in black, but sitting tall and statuesque. She, too, never shifted her attention from the cardinal. Raymond sighed softly, imperceptibly, and looked back to the front.

". . . and now I call up Jimmy's brother, Tommy, to say a few words."

Tommy rose and walked to the podium; the cardinal kissed him on both his cheeks, blessed him, then sat back on his chair, crosier in his hand. Tommy was tall, needing to hunch over a bit to be able to talk into the microphone. After a moment of feedback, he found the right distance from the mike head and began to recall, when they were both kids, how he and Jimmy had played cops and robbers. "I always wanted to be the bad guy," Tommy said. "And Jimmy always wanted to be the cop, like his Uncle Rick." Purses snapped open, and tissues were pulled from plastic packs; handkerchiefs were passed around; the sound of sniffles rippled quietly through the church, like a soft stone dropped into a warm calm pond. When Tommy finished, tears running down the sides of his cheeks, he went back to his seat, and the cardinal came back to the podium to finish the service.

The organ began playing as the mourners began to file out, row by row, like on a plane after a very rough flight.

Linda, Raymond, the rest of the family, and all the dignitaries filed out of the cathedral, and re-formed in a line outside. Once everyone was in place, the loudspeakers that were lined up and down Fifth Avenue broadcast the sound of a military-type command: "Present arms!" In unison, thousands of officers raised their right white-gloved hands in a military salute, while a sole bagpiper, standing on the front steps of the cathedral, began playing "Amazing Grace." Jimmy Kerrigan's body was lifted onto the shoulders of six uniformed New York City police officers, who walked it down the stairs of the cathedral. At the bottom of the stairs, the officers stopped in front of the cardinal, surrounded by six other priests, who lifted his aspergillum and sprinkled holy water on Jimmy's casket. The bagpiper finished his mournful song as the cardinal stepped to the side, while the ceremonial team loaded the flag-draped casket into the hearse and closed the door.

Another order barked over the loud speakers: "Order arms!" and the white gloves dropped to their side.

The commander of the ceremonial unit walked over to the mayor and said, in a hushed but affirmative tone, "On behalf of the family, thank you for being here." He looked at Raymond and Mrs. Kerrigan, Jimmy's veiled mother; then he took the mother by the arm and escorted her to the first limousine behind the hearse, Raymond following her into the car. The remainder of the family filled a dozen vehicles that followed directly in line. Once everyone was settled, 100 motorcycles, 60 from the NYPD and 40 from other city departments, began the deliberate ride to the Queens cemetery. Raymond watched out his window at the thousands of uniformed cops. He reached over to take Linda's hand.

He could feel his phone vibrating, and slipped it out of his jacket pocket. Sheilah had sent him a text: "Call me after six. I love you." He slid the phone back into the jacket and said nothing.

They arrived at the cemetery quickly, as all traffic on the route had been cleared in advance by hundreds of cops assigned to the funeral detail. The simple and moving ceremony lasted all of 30 minutes, and when it ended, Linda and many in her family broke down, their hands covering their mouths, their bodies jerking up and down. They each laid a single white rose on top of the casket. The cardinal ended the ceremony and thanked all the nonfamily for being there, and then blessed everyone.

As he walked back to his car, Raymond took Linda's hand once more, this time to lead her to the vehicle. In all his years in the New York City Police Department, and all the funerals that he had attended, this was the first time he felt shallow and empty. All the power his office held, all the strength he had, could do nothing for Linda and the family. It was only the second time in his career that he felt completely helpless, the other being September 11, 2001, the day when he lost his wife to a terrorist attack and when he watched dozens of people jump to their death, and there was nothing to do to help them. And yet as terrible as that day had been, this was now the worst day in his entire career.

CHAPTER 19

6:30 am, Tuesday, 24 October

Tuesday morning, before 6:30, he was back at his office. He made a cup of pod coffee for himself, with the machine he kept in his office for when Janey wasn't there. She brewed fresh in a real coffeepot she kept full and fresh all day.

He had changed there into one of several spare suits he kept in his closet. He would have his advance man head up to his apartment later that day to get some fresh clothes for the office.

The phone rang. He was expecting Jones, but it was Breshill on the other end. "Commissioner," he said into the phone.

"Yeah. What's up?" Raymond said. "It's still morning, isn't it? The bars close early last night?"

"I want to express my condolences for . . ."

Raymond cut him off. "Thanks. Appreciate it."

"Can we meet?" Breshill asked.

Oh Jesus, Raymond thought. What now? Then he said, "Where—and when?

"Lunch at noon at the bar in the Palace."

Raymond frowned to himself, took a deep breath, let the air out through his pursed lips, and said, "Okay. The Palace for lunch. I can use a drink. See you at 12." Raymond hung up the phone.

Breshill was already there, sitting in a corner of the softly lit bar that erased whatever time of day it was. It wasn't really a lunch place, which was why the room was mostly empty. The day bartender was busy setting up for the cocktail hour, at which time the Marcus bar would turn into Grand Central Terminal, only busier. When Raymond arrived, he slid into his side of the booth and waved off the waitress. "What's up?" he said to Breshill.

"First, let me express my condolences—"

"Thanks, but I know you didn't drag me up here for that. What's on your mind?"

"Commissioner, I mean it."

"Okay, thank you."

"Look, let me be straight with you. You've cut off my stream of sources, and there isn't a single cop in the NYPD who will talk to me, out of fear of being fired. My bosses are really pissed at me. I'm headed for the rapids."

"My heart's breaking."

"I need your help."

Raymond sighed. He waved the waitress back. He was ready for that drink. "Dewars," he said. "Neat. Soda back. What do you want?" he said to Breshill.

"Coffee, cream, two sugars."

She nodded her head and put a napkin down in front of Breshill, took away the half-empty bowl of cashew nuts that he had been working on, and replaced it with a fresh one.

"Listen carefully," the commissioner said. "You want my help? You do something for me. I want the head of the cell that's responsible for all these fucking attacks, the bastards who are responsible for my cops being shot in Times Square and Rock Center, and for the simultaneous attacks in North Carolina and Vegas."

Breshill had his spiral notebook out and clicked his Paper Mate, flipping pages back over themselves as he wrote everything down, grunting "uh-huh" every few seconds, as the waitress returned with their order. "I need to draw him out," Raymond began. "Into the open, to create a reason for him to move, or communicate, or pop his head out of his hole, and we believe that something's being planned for the city, but we have no fucking clue what it is."

"How do you know?" Breshill said as he took a loud sip of his coffee.

"I know," Raymond said. "We know. The FBI is sure, but neither of us knows when, how, or who."

Raymond's cell phone vibrated in his pocket. He answered it as he walked away from the table. When he returned, his demeanor had changed. "Scratch all that. I think we know who. That was Jones. She just gave me a name, Ibrahim Samadi. The Bureau believes he is the cell leader, out of Detroit."

"Is this on the record?"

"Not from me. Hell no! However, if you get the name from one of the Feds, it's all yours."

"How the fuck am I going to get it from them?" Breshill smirked.

"Jones doesn't know I'm talking to you. Call her right now and tell her that you heard from someone in the FBI wire room that they're looking for an Ibrahim Samadi. Tell her you're off the record, and when she admits it, you now have an anonymous senior FBI source."

Raymond went on, "He was in Detroit, but I think he might be here now. Where, exactly, we don't know yet, but we're closing the net around him."

Breshill looked at Raymond. "This is great. But why are you telling me?"

Raymond waited until the waitress put his drink down. "Because I want to send a message to Samadi and his fuckers that have done this. They killed my nephew. Now it's personal between him and me."

"Got it."

"It's fucking personal," Raymond repeated. "And, I cannot be your source for that name. But I want Samadi, dead or alive. I want to drag him through the streets of New York City by his dress."

Breshill was furiously scribbling into his notebook again, until Raymond put his hand on Breshill's and stopped him. "Don't print that dress thing. The rest of it you can have."

"I won't," Breshill said as he sipped the rest of his now cold and bitter coffee and took one more handful of cashews. "I can use the 'It's personal' statement, right?"

"Have a ball." Raymond downed his drink in one shot and got up to leave. "I'll pay for my drink; you pay for yours. Never want someone saying I was bought by a fucking reporter."

"Thanks Rick . . . Commissioner. Really, thank you!"

Not long after Raymond was back at the office, Janey buzzed his desk. When he answered her call, she said, "Agent Jones is on the phone, and she said it's important." He clicked over to Jones.

"We've got a fucking problem," she said crisply. Someone leaked Samadi's name to Breshill. He's got his name!"

Raymond tried to sound surprised. "How did he get it? What exactly does he have?"

"Samadi's name and that he's the cell leader operating in Detroit."

"Where do you think he got it?"

"He said the wire room, from one of ours, and since I couldn't lie and deny, I told him to just use an anonymous FBI source."

Perfect, Raymond thought.

"You know," Rick said, "He called and left a message for me to call him, saying it was important. He was probably looking for more intel. I'll return and see what he wants, and get back to you."

Raymond waited 15 minutes and called Jones back. "That's what he wanted," Raymond said. "I didn't confirm or deny either. Let's see what he prints."

Ten minutes later Breshill called Raymond's cell phone. When Raymond saw the call, he figured he was looking for something else. "Yeah, what's up?"

"Just wanted to say congratulations."

"For what? Did I hit the lottery or something?" Raymond said sarcastically.

"No sir, not the lottery. The grand jury's back. It's justifiable homicide."

"Really? How do you know?"

"Don't worry about that, but you didn't get it from me," and with that, Breshill hung up.

CHAPTER 20

6:50 am, Wednesday, 25 October

Raymond was awakened by his cell phone ringing on the table behind him. His head felt like it was stuffed with cotton, from sleeping on the couch in his private office.

"Yeah?"

"Boss, did you see the fucking news?" Gallagher said.

"No, what? Never mind, All the papers are on Janey's desk." He hung up, walked through his office, opened the door to Janey's, and grabbed Breshill's paper off her desk.

Fuck, he thought, as he picked it up and saw the front page:

IT'S PERSONAL, SAYS COMMISH
Story by Sammy Breshill starts on page 3

His cell started ringing again.

"You want to get yourself killed, is that it?" Jones said, sounding angry. "These guys aren't fucking around!"

"Listen to me," Raymond said, trying to hold on to the end of his short fuse, to keep it from going off. "He killed one of my cops. He tried to take out Rock Center, killed two of your guys, and my nephew, for fuck's sake. These fucking bastards attacked this city, destroyed the World Trade Center, and fucking killed my wife. They're like fucking chameleons, infiltrating our cities and communities. Look what they're doing to London, Paris, Germany for fuck's sake. What do you want me to do? Send Samadi a congratulatory telegram?"

He could hear Jones take a deep breath on the other end, before she spoke. "You sound like a fucking mad man."

"You know what? Go fuck yourself."

In what sounded like a quiet, stern, and suddenly, to Raymond, empathetic voice, Jones began talking softly. "Rick . . . we've been friends for a very long time. We've been through a lot together—good times and bad, but do not—I repeat—do not confuse my friendship for weakness. You are not above the law. You've been sworn to do a job, and you're going to do it to the letter of the law, or I swear to you, I will fucking lock you up myself." She paused to let all of that sink in. "I get that you're pissed off, and I'm sorry about Jimmy, but if you continue talking stupid and jeopardizing your safety and the safety of those around you, and jeopardizing this investigation, I will go to the mayor myself and call for your job. Do you understand, Commissioner? I'll see you at the Chambers Street Deli at ten for coffee, just as we had planned." Somehow, the empathy had evaporated by the end of her dressing down.

Raymond hung up the phone and sat there. He felt like he was losing control.

Just then, Gallagher walked in and looked at him.

"You okay?" Gallagher asked.

Raymond looked up at him. "Yes, I'm okay. I need a shower." He stood up and walked into his private office bathroom.

At 10 am, refreshed and with a new set of clothes, Raymond walked into the Chambers Street Deli, and went directly to the back where Jones was sitting at the far-end booth. He could smell her perfume, three booths earlier.

"I'm sorry about this morning," she said, sounding genuinely apologetic.

"Me too, but I'm trying to draw this guy out. I feel like he's fucking running us in circles."

"Listen to me, Rick. We're close. Very close. I know you want to kill this guy yourself, but it's going to be done right and by us. His trail went cold after Times Square, until we picked it up again, briefly, during Rock Center, then cold again until the last attacks. Between you and me, your cop collar, Hamadi, housed over at the Metropolitan Correctional Center, helped us get back on to Samadi. We need to stay on there now until we have a real ID, for him and every one of his sleepers. If he disappears and is replaced, we will lose them all. Our analysts believe they're planning this thing here, and it has something to do with Wall Street, and something up around Park and 65th, but we're not sure what." She looked at Raymond, and, for the first time, was concerned about the way he looked. "You getting any sleep?"

"This weekend I did," Raymond said. "I've cleared my schedule for this evening. I told Chief Allegra I'm shutting off my phone from 8 pm to 6 am, and not to bother me unless the world comes to an end." They both laughed. He knew Sheilah had a dinner to go to and would be out late, so he was going to catch up on his sleep.

"Okay," Jones said. "I've got a briefing this afternoon at three, so if we get something new, I'll give you a buzz."

"Good." They both stood up to leave, with Raymond throwing down a five dollar bill to cover his coffee. "Let's talk later."

Jones left the deli, and Raymond walked over to Archer, who was standing at the restaurant door, talking into the sleeve microphone, calling Shelby to bring the car to the door.

Raymond stepped out onto the sidewalk and into the back seat of the Suburban. He felt tired already. "Back to the office," he said. "I need a fucking nap." As he leaned back and closed his eyes, he thought of Jimmy lying in that casket, replayed arriving at Linda's home, and then thought of Sheilah. His mind was whirling, spinning everyone out of his thoughts but one. All that was left was Samadi. He picked up his phone and sent Breshill a text: "You're the fucking man! Keep the pressure on! RR."

That night, shortly after eleven, Sheilah let herself into her Brooklyn brownstone and switched on the living room light. When she and Raymond weren't bunkered down at the Marcus, and she had the time, it was nice to get back home. She was dead tired, having attended a B'nai B'rith dinner, and she was thirsty. All that salty food made her want a bottle of cold water from the fridge. She had put on her public face for the event and wore her running-for-mayor-someday clothes. She knew the men at the event liked her; men always liked her wherever she went—that was easy. But so did the women, because she always came off charismatically smart and charming, never condescending. These perceptions would come in handy when she ran for mayor—whenever that might be.

She took off her gray Armani suit jacket and casually let it drop to the floor. She headed for the kitchen to get the water, and also put the kettle on for a late-night cup of chamomile, to help her fall asleep more quickly.

That's when she noticed the odd smell.

Her first thought was that her housekeeper forgot to take out the garbage. She would have to talk to her about that, and other things. Lately there had been a lot of little . . .

The thick, hairy, sweaty arm that came around her neck from behind took her totally by surprise. She tried to scream, but the arm had effectively choked off her vocal cords; nothing came out. She stood, paralyzed and panicky, as she felt a canvas hood being placed roughly over her head. In one move, it completely covered her down to her neck. She screamed again, but the hood was so tight against her mouth, she sounded as if she were underwater. She could barely breathe at all, and when she did try to take a deep breath, the dust from the bag caused her to choke. She could feel the canvas now sticking to her face, which was already drenched with sweat.

She felt a set of hands pull her arms behind her and tightly bind her wrists, one crossed over the other, as she felt a stinging sensation around her wrists, the thick plastic zip ties cutting into her flesh.

Her mind flashed on Rick playing one of their games, until she felt the cold rise from her legs straight up to her brain. She wiggled involuntarily to shake off the chill. She tried to move her wrists, but the more she moved, the more the plastic cut into them, and her fingers were starting to tingle.

One of them finally spoke. The voice was rough, her lawyer mind noted, and his accent meant that he was not American. "I remove your hood. Do not make sound."

She shook her head up and down quickly. He grabbed the hood from the top and pulled it off in one swift motion. She felt like her head was going with it. In the dark of her apartment, she could see the shadows of three men, all wearing black masks and black clothing.

"Please," she said. In response, a hand smacked her hard across her face. Her left cheek felt hot. She dropped her head in surrender, hoping whatever was coming would happen quickly and they would leave.

One of the men standing to her side grabbed her hair and yanked her head up and back; another one slapped duct tape across her mouth, and wound the tape twice around her head and under her hair. When she felt the one let go of her hair, she dropped her head down again. The men started talking to each other rapidly in a language she didn't understand; it took her a few seconds to realize it was possibly Arabic. Her heart pounded like a hammer hitting an anvil.

No . . .

Standing at the far end of the living room, two of the men grabbed her arms, one man on each side of her, and forced her down to her knees, facing away from the kitchen. They let go of her, threatening what would happen if she dared to move. She could hear a lot of movement behind her, but could not tell what they were doing. Working methodically, one man placed a small chair at the other end of the room in front of a large bookshelf, and the other set up a tripod with a small camera on it, about five feet in front of the chair, facing it. The third man unfolded an ISIS black flag and hung it on the bookshelf directly behind the chair. Then two of the men went back to Sheilah, putting an arm on each side of her; they stood her up and turned her around toward the chair. For a few seconds she was confused, but then she realized what was happening, and her knees went limp, and she nearly fainted.

They dragged her over to the chair, sat her up straight, and turned on a lamp on the camera. The man with the sweaty arms stood to her right, holding a 16-inch scimitar. Moving in back of Sheilah so he was standing directly behind her, he waved the sword at the camera and shouted, "*We are coming for you! You cannot avoid or resist us. We will show you no mercy!*" He then moved out of camera range and came back with a towel. He wiped the sweat and tears off Sheilah's face with it. He then held up the front page of the *New York Herald* with the headline "*IT'S PERSONAL, SAYS COMMISSIONER*" and taped it to her chest. The other two men stood on each side of her, holding her in place.

No, no. Please, no . . .

The man with the scimitar pulled her back against the chair, as she closed her eyes tight and held her breath. The last thing Sheilah felt was the blade start to slide across her neck.

The three men laughed when her upper torso lurched forward, causing a stream of blood to shoot across the room, while the sword-wielding murderer stood there holding her head. All three yelled "*Allahu Akbar*" several times; then one shut the camera off, took the SIM card out, turned off the lamp on the camera, and packed everything into a hard suitcase. With their mission accomplished, they left quietly through the front door of Sheilah's brownstone, down the staircase to the dark Brooklyn street, and walked casually into the night, talking and laughing among themselves with what seemed like not a care in the world.

CHAPTER 21

7:15 am, Thursday, 26 October

Raymond got to the office just after seven. He loved getting there before everyone else got in . . . no headaches, calls, meetings, nothing except catching up on paperwork and reading at his own pace, usually without interruption. He was at his desk sipping the mug of coffee that he had just brewed from the coffeepot that Janey set up for him yesterday before she left for the day. He had not heard from Sheilah the night before, but knew she had an event to go to, and also knew she made a habit of staying off her phone at those events. She must have gotten home and crashed. Wanting to touch base with her this morning, he called her cell, and when it went right to voice mail, he called the landline in her brownstone; still no response. Then he called the Marcus, but nothing. Maybe she's at the gym, he thought.

About 8:15, he tried calling her again, several times, but there was no answer. This wasn't like Sheilah, he thought.

He took a sip of the hot black coffee, then checked his schedule for Monday. Meetings with several police officers, lunch with City Council, three o'clock appearance with the mayor in East Harlem to dedicate who the fuck knows what, cocktails at five with the governor and the mayor at Gracie Mansion . . . He closed his appointment book and rubbed his eyes and laughed out loud as he read through the reports in front of him. A male sergeant and female detective had gotten caught in flagrante delicto. When a duty captain on night watch rolled up on them, on a dead-end street, the sergeant jumped out of his car and, while fixing his pants, explained to the captain that the detective's mother had been diagnosed with cancer, and he was actually consoling her. Raymond wondered how the captain kept a straight face while speaking to the sergeant. This will be interesting, he thought.

Suddenly, he could hear a lot of movement outside his door, and then he heard the sound of the buzzer for the outer corridor doors controlled by the detectives assigned to security for the commissioner's office. He heard Gallagher's door to the hallway open and close about five times . . . so much that he was now annoyed and stood up to see what the hell was going on. He was midway between his desk and the door when it burst open. Gallagher and Jones walked in, and Raymond could see a half-dozen suits behind them in the hallway.

"What the hell is going on?" he asked.

Gallagher, standing there looking like he was about to vomit, said, "Commissioner, please sit down."

"Sit down, Rick," Jones repeated. Raymond slowly sat at his desk, staring at the two of them, realizing that something was very seriously wrong. The first thing he thought of was his sister Linda, or maybe it was another attack.

He watched Jones open the small yellow envelope she was holding, take a SIM card from it, and slip it into the side of Raymond's computer. The two came around and stood behind the commissioner. The movie app popped onto the screen, and Jones hit the play button. Gallagher put his hands on Raymond's shoulders as the video began.

Nobody said anything as the video played until the assassin grabbed Sheilah's head and brought the scimitar up to her neck. Gallagher reached down and punched the eject button. Raymond looked up at Gallagher, noticeably shaking.

"She's dead, Rick," Gallagher said. Jones looked at Gallagher and waved her hands for him to stop talking.

Raymond slid off the chair and fell to his knees, and then stood up, holding onto the desk for support, his face like a wounded bear's.

"Commissioner," Gallagher said. "Commissioner," he repeated, as Raymond just stood there, as if he didn't even see Jones or him. Jones's eyes filled with tears . . . she could feel his pain.

"I'll be right back," Raymond said. Jones and Gallagher tried to stop him, but he shook them off like they were rain on a twisting umbrella. "I'll be right back," he said again.

Raymond went into his private bathroom. Gallagher and Jones looked at each other for a few seconds as they heard him puking as if he had been on a three-day drunk. He was in there for close to 15 minutes. When he walked out, his face was red, and his eyes were swollen like he had been crying for days.

Almost as if he had been hypnotized, not hearing anything they were saying, Raymond walked right by them, to Archer in the hallway, said, "Let's go," and started walking to the elevator. Gallagher went up to him. "Listen, Commissioner," he urged, "why don't you sit down for a minute."

Raymond just stared at him, then continued walking and got on the elevator with Archer; as the doors closed, Gallagher locked eyes with Archer, put his hand up to his right ear, like he was holding a phone, and mouthed, "Call me."

Shelby was sitting in the Suburban as Archer held the door open and Raymond got in. Shelby looked back at the commissioner and said, "Where to, Boss?"

"To the Marcus," Raymond said, just staring ahead.

Archer started to panic . . . what the fuck is he going to do, he thought to himself. Without picking up the phone so Raymond could see it, he texted Gallagher, telling him where they were going. Gallagher wrote back, "Do not leave him alone."

When they arrived at the Marcus, Raymond sat in the car in front of the entrance, just staring at the hotel through the black-tinted glass of the SUV for several minutes, while Shelby and Archer sat in the front, growing more uncomfortable by the minute. After about 10 minutes, Archer got up enough courage to speak, "Boss, you okay?"

"Yeah. Head down to 51st and Madison."

Shelby put the vehicle in drive and slowly pulled away. Archer then sent Gallagher another text message: "We're on the way to 51st and Madison. I think he's going to St. Pat's."

Gallagher replied, "Is he okay?"

"Not sure. He hasn't said a word. We just sat in front of the Marcus. I'll let you know when we get to 51 and Mad."

"Received," Gallagher wrote.

Twenty minutes later, Shelby pulled up to 51st and Madison, behind St. Patrick's Cathedral, and put the Suburban in park. He looked back at Raymond, sleeping, his head leaning against the window. Archer put his finger up to his mouth, motioning for Shelby not to say anything. They sat there for about 15 minutes, until all of a sudden, Raymond was out of the car. Archer jumped out and walked about one step to the right and behind as Raymond turned left on 51st Street, toward the cardinal's residency at the rectory. He walked up to the door and rang the bell. In a few minutes a priest answered, looking surprised that the police commissioner was standing there. The priest invited him in. Raymond thanked him and said, "I don't need to see the cardinal; I just need some time to pray." The priest felt a little uncomfortable. He could see that Raymond was upset. He escorted him to one of the first side pews in the front of the cathedral. On a Monday morning, the church wasn't packed, but this area was always roped up for security reasons. Raymond sat by himself, and Archer stood about 20 feet behind him.

Forty-five minutes went by, with Raymond deep in prayer. Finally, Gallagher and Jones entered the cathedral, walked toward him, got to his row, and sat on either side of him. Gallagher spotted a pistol in Raymond's hand that he was holding out of sight. It was his off-duty weapon that he usually carried in an ankle holster. Gallagher reached down slowly and took it out of Raymond's hand. Raymond offered no resistance. Without looking at either man, he put his head down and sobbed.

CHAPTER 22

6:15 pm, Thursday, 26 October

Gallagher and Archer arrived with Raymond back at his apartment in Riverdale. He and Archer then stayed there for the evening. The next morning, Raymond was up early and joined Gallagher and Archer, already in the kitchen having coffee. Raymond was trained to sleep lightly, and the slightest sound automatically made him sit up and reach for his gun in one motion, but when his head hit the pillow that night, he didn't move until he got out of bed the next morning.

Gallagher said, "How are you feeling, Boss? Shelby's in the Suburban outside."

He ignored the question. "I can't find my fucking phone," he said. "I need to get to the office. I need to get my head straight, and catch up on all kinds of paperwork shit."

Gallagher just stared at him. "I've got your phone; it was ringing and pinging all night long."

"Who was it? Let me have it."

"Listen," Gallagher said, "I spoke to Jones about four times, as well as your sister, the mayor, the governor, and the president's chief of staff. They all called to see how you were doing. There were a few dozen other calls that I didn't entertain—you can get back to them later."

"Okay, let me have it. Where is it?" Raymond said as he went to the counter in the kitchen to turn on the television.

Gallagher jumped up from the table and turned off the television before the picture could come on. He moved so quickly, he startled both Raymond and Archer, who was sitting there quietly feeling uncomfortable watching and listening to Gallagher handle his boss.

"No TV," Gallagher said. "You really don't need to see it. It's on every fucking station—local, cable, international—everywhere. As for your phone, let me hold onto it. The Google alert you have on your name dumped more than 7,000 notifications to your phone in the past 12 hours. Besides headlining every U.S. newspaper, Sheilah's death is on the front page of the *Hong Kong Press*, the *London News*, and the *Australian Press*, and you're mentioned in just about every story."

Raymond sat there staring at the table. His eyes filled with tears. Archer got up and signaled to Gallagher that he'd be outside in the SUV.

"Listen," Gallagher said, "the next five or six days are going to be rough. Really rough! I've spoken to Sheilah's family, and she will be laid out in St. Pat's from 12 pm to 9 pm on Monday, and with the funeral on Tuesday at 10 am. Our ceremonial unit's handling the entire thing. Jet Blue is flying her family in from around the country, and we expect every major prosecutor in the country up to the

U.S. attorney general. Lastly, I took the liberty to tell the mayor that you're going to be out for the next two weeks. After the funeral, you need to get out of here for a few days and decompress."

Raymond sat there staring into space. "Okay," he finally said. "You're right. Let's go down to the office. I need to see the mayor and speak to Jones."

He threw some clothes on, and together they stepped outside. To Raymond's surprise, a four-car motorcade was waiting outside. Instead of his SUV and a backup, there were lead and follow marked highway units, and the backup Suburban was switched out to an ESU truck with a counterterrorism team that would now be the backup vehicle, but unlike two detectives, these guys were armed to the teeth . . . looking like they were headed for Iraq.

"What's this?" he said.

"The first dep has increased your detail until we get these fuckers."

Archer met Raymond at his Suburban, opened the door, and closed it behind him. He got in, and off they rode. Gallagher jumped into his department car and followed the motorcade. Before he pulled out, he sent Archer a text message: "Do not let him out of your sight. I'm right behind you."

Forty-five minutes later, they pulled into the garage at headquarters, and although they had been there only yesterday, Gallagher thought to himself, it seemed like a year.

Every 15 minutes, Gallagher came up with an excuse to walk into Raymond's office. Just after 1 pm, he did it again, this time to ask Raymond if he wanted something to eat. He found Raymond sitting in his chair staring at the wall.

"Commissioner, you hungry?"

"I killed her," Raymond said evenly, without moving.

"You didn't kill her. ISIS killed her. This guy Samadi killed her; his guys killed her. You did not kill her."

"Because of that stupid headline." He looked up at Gallagher. "I did this."

"No, you didn't. They did. Now you have to concentrate on getting Samadi and his gang of thugs. Don't sit around feeling sorry for yourself. It won't help you get them."

"She's gone. Jerry."

"Yeah, she's gone, but don't let her death be in vain. You've got to focus on Samadi."

Raymond said nothing for a long time, then stood up. "I need to get cleaned up." As he headed for his private bathroom, he turned and looked at Gallagher. The fire had returned to Raymond's eyes. "He'll pay."

Over the next few days, Sheilah's death and the investigation by the FBI and NYPD were front-page news all over the world. Raymond did everything in his power to be as invisible as he could, but the press was hot and heavy, one minute reflecting on the gruesome way Sheilah was murdered by the terrorists, Sheilah's life in public serice, and the next minute raising questions about her relationship with Raymond. The only thing that kept the press from tipping the scale against Raymond was a constant barrage of articles put out by Breshill on Raymond and on his and the FBI's hunt for Samadi, ISIS, and the guys that killed Sheilah.

On the morning of Sheilah's funeral, more than 15,000 cops, prosecutors, and judges lined up on Fifth Avenue, with six helicopters hovering overhead, and with unparalleled security. The governor, mayor, and U.S. attorney general spoke. Raymond was asked, but just couldn't do it. By that evening when they put her in the ground, Raymond felt like the day had lasted a year. He was glad it was over.

The next morning at 7:30, Raymond, Archer, and three detectives from the Intelligence Division boarded a jet for Denver. For the next two-and-a-half weeks, Raymond adopted the schedule of a world-class prize fighter in training. Daily workouts, runs, and hikes that would have killed most men half his age. He was on a mission, and he could hardly wait to get back to get started.

CHAPTER 23

8:15 pm, Monday, 20 November

Raymond walked into his office for the first time in three weeks, feeling like a different person. He had lost about 15 pounds and looked great. Although he spoke to his office and Jones daily, there was still a ton of catch-up to do, and he jumped right in.

Later in the following week, the U.S. attorney general, the FBI director, and Jones convened a two-day major intel briefing in Washington, D.C. All the key players were in attendance—the FBI, the CIA, the State Department, the D.C. police, and the NYPD, represented by Rick Raymond and a half-dozen New York City police executives. Normally, Raymond would not attend anything like this, but given that the AG and the FBI director were speaking, he didn't have a choice. He knew that everyone was watching him, and that Gallagher thought he was losing it—that he was some sort of ticking time bomb. He also heard that the mayor had been asking his criminal justice coordinator how he was doing, and said he had concerns Rick may be obsessed with Sheilah's death and lacked focus on managing the day-to-day operation of the NYPD—50,000 strong—not to mention the everyday problems of securing the city.

The purpose of this meeting was for everybody to compare notes, to review everything that had happened, to see if there was anything they might have missed.

They sat around a huge table, with giant screens hung above, for illustration. Jones sat at one end, behind a podium, as they went over the events of the attacks—Times Square, Rockefeller Center, North Carolina, Las Vegas. What had they had missed? What had they overlooked? Had any clue slipped by them unnoticed? Why, Jones had pondered for days, did they not see those attacks coming? Again she thought, what did they miss? And what could they learn from what happened? They had dusted Sheilah's apartment for prints and come up with nothing. No bloody footprints, no hairs, no fibers from clothes. Nothing. They canvassed the neighbors. Nothing. In Las Vegas, they checked all the security cameras. Nothing had survived the blast. And the witnesses that survived gave them nothing usable. It all happened too fast. They had the body of the shooter in North Carolina; they identified him as an operative of a cell the FBI already had its eye on, and had hit during the raid that had killed Jimmy. But, in spite of everything, they had very little to go on about Samadi, other than he liked to work in twos—two cops shot in Times Square; two cities hit at the same time.

Jones had led the review, and, when she was finished, said, "We're now going to have a report by Mila Chernova, the supervising FBI agent assigned to the New York City Joint Terrorism Task Force. She has been working with us since we discovered Bakheer's house in Paterson, New Jersey. She will tell us why she believes the next targets are Wall Street and a Hebrew school in Upper Manhattan. Agent Chernova?" Jones nodded for her to come to the podium.

Mila stood up, and as she walked to the podium, everyone made note of her commanding presence.

She was tall, with black hair pulled back tight against her head and swirled behind. She had dark eyes, flawless porcelain skin, and strong shoulders. She had a white shirt on that was buttoned to the top, and a pants suit that went all the way down to her black heels. Not an inch of skin besides her face and her long-fingered hands was visible but, clearly, her physique was powerful. She had worked on several important cases, and was known in the Bureau for her obsessiveness when she worked on them. It was not uncommon for her to put in 14-hour days in front of her computer, feeding in information and analyzing the results. She was methodical, dedicated, unrelenting; and all of that rolled up together produced an attention to detail that bordered on the scary. As far as Jones knew, she didn't have much of a personal life; she didn't do anything except work on cases and go to the gym, usually at five in the morning, for a full workout before she arrived at her office at seven.

Raymond was into her immediately, but not only for her feminine pulchritude. She was going to help him get Samadi.

Raymond stayed at the Fairmont in downtown D.C. with his two bodyguards, and the rest of the NYPD contingency were at the Melrose. The first night, after the conference session ended, Raymond had a drink with Gallagher at the hotel bar, then retreated to his room. This was an energized group of people, and they were ready to party hearty in D.C., where it was practically mandatory to get plastered until 3 am. Those who didn't were considered to be wimps. For Rick, there were no parties, no horsing around. He ate alone in his room, was in bed by nine, and slept hard and deep, his body refueling for the big fight he knew was coming.

The second day was much like the first, with most of the talking done by Chernova. For close to two hours, she went over cell phone data, cell site/tower locations, and the correlation of cell phones they believed were used by Samadi and his crew. Tracking his communications bouncing back and forth from Detroit and New York, as well as tracking six other phones that were floating around in Manhattan's Upper East Side, Wall Street, and Atlantic Avenue in Brooklyn. She passed out charts to everyone, and used projected maps to show why she thought which school was going to be hit, and when, and how the terrorists were going to try to blow up the stock exchange. Although it was quite technical and many in the room appeared lost, the NYPD officers were impressed as much by her presence as her presentation. Everyone listened, took notes, asked questions, and nothing happened.

Two hours into the presentation, although riveted by Mila's presentation, Raymond knew he had to get back to New York City before the official ending of the briefing. The mayor's going to kill me, he thought to himself. Right after lunch break, Raymond made his rounds to say his goodbyes to the people in the room. He got to Mila when she was talking to a few D.C. cops while having a cup of coffee. He shook her hand in thanks and handed her his business card. In response, she pulled hers out of a pocket in her short black blazer, took out a pen, and wrote her cell number on the back.

"Call me if you need anything," she said.

"You do the same," he said, trying to maintain his professionalism as he felt a sudden attraction.

Jones, Raymond, and his bodyguards, luggage in tow, walked together to Union Station and boarded an Amtrak Acela at noon. At 3:15 that Friday afternoon, Raymond stepped off the elevator on the 14th floor of One Police Plaza and walked into his office . . . back to the real world.

Eight o'clock that evening, Archer dropped Raymond off at Gallagher's home. Raymond joined Gallagher down in the family room for a drink, and the two discussed a number of department issues that Gallagher had been dealing with over the last two days. He also mentioned that he received a call from the mayor's chief of staff asking how Raymond was doing. They both agreed that in the morning Raymond should spend some time with the mayor to ensure him all was good. Hey, Saturday morning would be perfect.

No one around, no prayers at City Hall, no rumors, no BS. Gallagher immediately called the sergeant in charge of the mayor's security detail and told him that the sooner the police commissioner could see the mayor the better. Ten minutes later, the sergeant called back.

The meeting was set for the following day, 9:00 am, at Gracie Mansion.

CHAPTER 24

5:00 pm, Monday, 4 December

Jones and Raymond, accompanied by Archer and driven by Shelby in Raymond's black Suburban, arrived at the Metropolitan Correctional Center, the federal detention center otherwise known as the MCC. A few minutes from NYPD police headquarters, the MCC remained one of the most tightly guarded federal holding facilities in the United States. Shelby pulled into the private driveway, and Archer got out first. Jones and Raymond jumped out of the back and walked toward the lobby.

"You gonna tell me what we're doing here?" Raymond asked Jones.

"Mila will tell you," she said, adding, "It was her idea."

Over the past week, Jones and FBI agent Chernova had been speaking to Raymond daily about their attempts to figure out what Samadi and his crew were up to next, and how to ID and stop them.

Late in the evening the night before, Chernova had called and told him she had an idea that she was going to run by Jones and the assistant U.S. attorney who was overseeing the federal investigation. Raymond asked what it was, but Chernova had said she couldn't tell him until she'd gotten approval.

"Don't you know I'm the New York City police commissioner?" Raymond said, more joking than challenging, to which Chernova responded, without missing a beat, "So, Commissioner, you're going to tie me down and torture it out of me?" Raymond laughed and said, "No comment," as his mind raced: was she referring to police brutality or was she flirting? He chose to keep it professional.

Now, stepping into the lobby, Raymond saw her, and his mind raced back to the "no-go" zone. She looked fantastic in her fitted beige pants suit. A federal corrections lieutenant told them to go back outside and leave their firearms in their vehicles. Jones and Raymond did as they were asked.

"Crack the gate," the lieutenant barked into a radio, and the huge metal gates slid from left to right. The three of them walked through the first floor, into an elevator that took them to the ninth floor, where former New York City police officer Hamadi was being held, along with the most deadly and violent prisoners. When the doors opened, they were met by four corrections officers that looked like linemen for the New York Giants.

The lieutenant led the way, and the four COs followed the group down an airless gray hallway, into an area marked "Attorney/Client Visits" that had a number of cubicles enclosed by two-inch bullet-proof glass. The internal speakers in the booth allowed visitors to speak to someone on the other side.

The lieutenant unlocked one of the large cubicles and told them to have a seat. Once they were inside, the door was locked behind them. Even with all his time in the business, the sound of metal against metal felt uncomfortable to Raymond.

The lieutenant told them Hamadi would be there soon.

Almost two minutes passed before they heard a loud bang in the distance, the sound of a prison door slamming open and then being slammed shut. All of a sudden, this massive metal wall slid open left to right, and there was Hamadi. He was surrounded by five uniformed officers, one on each side, three behind him. He was handcuffed to a chain that was wrapped around his waist, from which another chain was locked onto the shackles on both his feet. He was dressed in an orange prison jumpsuit with "DOC" in thick black letters written across the back. He was unshaven, his hair covered by a hairnet that reached all the way to underneath his chin, which Raymond realized was a spit mask that prevented him from spritzing bodily fluids on anyone. He looked emaciated; either they weren't feeding him, or, more likely, he was refusing to eat. The three of them watched Hamadi take baby steps, his legs restricted by his shackles, toward the adjoining cubicle. His cuffs were removed, and he was waist-chained to his chair.

Hamadi removed the spit mask from his face and said hello.

Chernova did the speaking as Jones and Raymond sat there listening and studying Hamadi. Jones thought to herself, there's no way I could live like this for the rest of my life. I would kill myself.

Chernova began: "I'm Mila Chernova, special agent for the FBI." She could see him studying her face, and then his eyes going down her body. She knew he hadn't seen a woman since the day he was arrested.

Hamadi nodded.

"How are you doing?" she said.

Again, he nodded.

"Look, I want to talk to you. I know what it's like in there. You're in special isolation 23 hours a day, no radio, no TV, no newspapers, no nothing. You measure your days by the crap they serve you for food."

"It's not food. It's dog shit," he muttered.

That's what she wanted, to engage him, to get him to start talking.

"I'm sorry." She leaned forward, making sure he could see the outline of her breasts. She watched his eyes go to them, then back to her. He was hungry, all right. "Look, Victor . . . Is it okay if I call you Victor?" She let her voice get a little huskier. He nodded his head yes.

"You're going to live like this until the day you die; you know that, right?"

He shook his head up and down.

"I need some information from you. If you cooperate, I've been given the authority to offer you a deal, and that deal would allow you to be deported to Egypt. You'd get to go home."

He put his head in his hands, and his whole body shook up and down.

"In order for this to happen, you must cooperate fully. Do you understand?"

He nodded. His eyes widened; she could see he was interested and engaged.

"Is this something you're willing to do?"

"Yes, ma'am."

"Samadi, the man you and the others worked for, the guy in Detroit . . . who is he?"

He looked up at her and stared directly into her eyes. "I don't know this man as Samadi." He paused. "I know him as Hashem; that's all. I spoke to him by burners that we changed every three weeks."

Chernova took a deep breath. Fuck, she thought, another name. For the next 25 minutes, she queried him about the other accomplices, locations, vehicles, etc. . . . everything she already knew the answers to, all in an attempt to see if he was telling the truth. She was convinced he was.

She looked at him and said, "Okay. I believe you're being truthful, but I need more. I need to know how to find Samadi, or Hashem . . . How do I find him?"

"We communicated through a Gmail account, a Gmail address. We never sent any emails through the account, but would draft a message and save it until the other party read it. The other party has the account and password information. They open the saved Gmail, read it, and then delete it. Then I would write an email on my end, to the same account, then save it without sending. No one detects it because nothing is ever sent."

Now Chernova burned her eyes into him. "Victor, we found that Gmail address in your computer, but it doesn't appear to have been used. I need more or I can't get you back to Egypt."

"If you subpoena Gmail/Google, ask them for the IP address that signed into the account. You'll find mine, which you already have from my computer, and another one that belongs to Hashem in Detroit. That's how you can find him. When you find his IP address, you'll find the others that he was talking to as well. Most of us didn't know each other. Everyone acted independently until a mission was ordered. The guys I was with, I didn't meet until two weeks before the mission."

"Brilliant," Chernova said softly. Then, going against the government's policy of never telling your source what you know, she decided to give it a shot. "Listen, we believe something's going to happen in New York City soon, and Samadi's speaking to four to eight others. How do we find them?"

"The IP addresses, if you can get them, but also, even if they're using burners, on Fridays they'll all be sent to a travel agency on Atlantic Avenue, at the corner of Smith, to pick up money. They're given money orders."

"Are you sure?" Mila said, trying to reserve her excitement.

"I'm positive. Video the surveillance there, and monitor the phones that come and go from there. You'll get the guys talking to him."

Mila just stared at him, "Anything else?" she asked.

"I can go back to Egypt, right?"

"Yes, if this works out, you'll go, I promise."

With that, she banged on the door and the team of officers came to let herself, Raymond, and Jones out of the cubicle, to be escorted down to the first floor. As they arrived at the first-floor lobby waiting for clearance to leave the building, Jones and Raymond congratulated Chernova on how she had handled Hamadi. Raymond held up his hand to give her a high five. She quietly leaned toward him so Jones could not hear, and said, "Well, now that you know my idea, I guess we'll have to find another excuse for you to tie me down." Before he could say anything, she brushed her hand across a dozen pair of handcuffs that were hanging in the office where they were being held for clearance. "These could be quite helpful," she snapped, and immediately turned and walked away from him.

Raymond said goodbye to Jones and Chernova and got into his Suburban. The two women walked over to FBI headquarters. Once there, Chernova went to work on her computer, and Jones assigned a team of agents to start subpoenaing Google.

Raymond was back at Police Plaza. He called the mayor to brief him, returned about 20 calls to union heads, members of the City Council, and his executive staff, and signed off on a couple of dozen notifications that he was being sued—he averaged about 20 a day. He sat back in his chair, thinking of what a productive day he had, how helpful Hamadi was.

He leaned back and closed his eyes. All he could see was Mila doing her thing with Hamadi.

Something about this woman was getting to him.

CHAPTER 25

9:55 am, Tuesday, 5 December

Looking a little concerned, Gallagher came out of his office and approached the commissioner's desk. Raymond said, "What's up?"

"I just got a call from an attorney who wants to come see you about Sheilah. He refused to tell me what he wanted, but insisted he needed to see you privately and that you should have an attorney with you."

"Fuck, what's this about?" Raymond said, feeling a knot in his stomach. "Get him back on the phone and tell him to come see me today at noon."

Gallagher said okay and then asked, "What do you want to do about a lawyer for yourself?"

"I don't need a fucking lawyer," he laughed. "Let's see what he wants."

Raymond sat back in the chair, and his mind was racing. What now?

It was just before eleven when Raymond's cell phone rang. It was Jones, with Chernova on an extension from another phone. "We have the subpoenas," Chernova said, then added, "And we have what you want. It looks like the IP address belongs to the guy in Detroit. He is now using a new email address, but they're definitely using the same method of sharing messages by not sending emails through the system. Very clever. We have also ID'd one principal phone we believe is Samadi's and seven others that call him twice every day, once at 10 am and once at 5 pm."

"Do you have a location in Detroit for us?" Jones asked.

"We don't think he's in Detroit anymore ," Chrenova said, "but it seems now he's in New York."

"Really? Where exactly? Do we know?"

"We've been on the device several times," Chrenova said. "However, he keeps the device shut off, and deactivates to a location device. The few times he's turned the device on, it's been from a different location. The last time a Starbucks in Downtown Manhattan, on Broadway, just across from Wall Street. That's the same area where a few of the phones have been calling from." Beads of sweat covered Raymond's forehead, and sweat from his underarms stained his shirt with what looked like pairs of half-moons.

Jones thanked Chernova and said she was calling an emergency meeting of the Joint Terrorism Task Force first thing in the morning. "Let's get these guys."

"I'll see you there," Chernova said. Raymond assumed she was talking to the both of them.

"I've got a 7 am with the mayor and an 11 am City Council hearing, but I'm free after that," he said.

Jones finished with, "We've got a team putting together additional affidavits for Title III intercepts, and we're working with DOJ DC on the FISA for anything we find."

"Okay," Raymond said. "I'll call you guys after my meeting with the City Council," and he hung up. Not 30 seconds later, his cell rang again. It had to be Chernova, because her caller ID number was the only one that ever showed up on his phone as all zeros.

"Yes?" he said.

"So, what are you doing for dinner?" she asked. Her voice was softer than it sounded during the official call. Raymond felt a sudden wave of warmth roll down the front of his body.

"I planned on going home early, so I figured I'd have something there."

"You want to meet me in Manhattan somewhere?"

First he thought of the Marcus, but couldn't bring himself to go there. "Listen, pick a place downtown and I'll just meet you there."

"Great, there's a small Italian place called Antonio's, on 44th and 12th, around the corner from my apartment. I'll see you there. About seven?"

"Done. I'll see you there."

Just as he hung up, Gallagher walked in to let him know that the lawyer was here to see him. Gallagher laughed and said, "I'm not sure what he wants, but his briefcase costs more than my fucking car."

"Just bring him in," Raymond snapped.

Gallagher escorted the attorney into the office, and Raymond got up and introduced himself.

"Commissioner," the attorney began, "I'm Paul Steene, and I work for Leonard White and Noble. I'm handling Sheilah Dannis's estate. Do you have a lawyer here?"

Raymond knew the firm, one of the biggest in the city, but was confused about what he would have to do with Sheilah's estate and why he would have an attorney. "No, I wanted to find out what this is all about first."

"Commissioner, on the evening of Monday, October 23, Ms. Dannis came to our office and updated her trust and her will. The reason I'm here today is because a substantial portion of her considerable fortune concerns you directly. She left one third of her estate to the New York Fallen Officers Fund, one third to a 9/11 Victims Charity in the name of your wife Mary, and one third of her fortune to you personally. That's about $33 million for you.

Raymond was in a daze . . . Monday evening was the day of Jimmy's funeral; it was after they spent the weekend together at the Marcus. What was she thinking, he wondered; she was killed just two days later. How could this be?

"I'm not sure what to say," Raymond said. "I'm a little confused."

"Commissioner, I wanted you to have a copy of her trust documents and will. You'll want to sit down with an attorney and go through this, as there are obvious tax implications that you'll need to deal with, but I thought you should know sooner than later."

With that, Steene excused himself and left the office, and Raymond just sat at the edge of his desk staring out the window. Gallagher walked back in after escorting the attorney to the elevator. "What just happened?" Raymond said softly under his breath.

Later that evening, Raymond sat down alone in a booth at the back of Antonio's, the restaurant that Mila recommended. The smell of garlic overwhelmed him, and as he looked around the place, he felt like he was in a scene from *The Godfather*, or in a real-life family restaurant on the outskirts of Rome. Sitting in the back, with his back facing the wall, was an old habit of his that he retained from his detective days; he never sat with his back toward the door. The seat's red leather smelled like the interior of a used Mercedes.

Antonio's wasn't completely empty. There were several people drinking at the bar, mostly men in pinstripe suits, alone, looking down at their drinks, and one or two well-dressed women, sitting by themselves, their dresses a little too short and their heels a little too high, sipping champagne and working their iPhones. The bartender brought them their drinks without asking, Raymond noticed, so he figured it was a work night for the ladies as well as for the bartender.

The waitress came over and put a napkin down in front of him. "Can I bring you something?" Her voice sounded to him like a spoonful of sugar.

"Yeah," he said. "Scotch. Dewars. Neat. Soda back. Make it a double. The Scotch, not the soda."

"Double D soda back," she sang, like it was a lyric to a song. He watched her glide back to the service end of the bar; he didn't notice the tall, dark-haired woman coming over to him.

"Anyone sitting here?" Chernova asked, as she put her palm on his shoulder, nodding to the empty part of the seat next to him. She was wearing a tight blue skirt and a white, tight-fitting tank top under a blue jacket.

"You are," he said smiling, waving with his hand for her to sit. She slid in beside him and nodded over to the waitress, who floated over and took her order of a glass a Prosecco. "One Pro," the waitress said, smiling, before turning back and heading for the bar.

After a brief stretch of silence, Chernova said, "So, what's for dinner?" Before he could answer, her Prosecco came. She took a sip from her glass, leaving an impression on it of her red lips, like fingerprints. "Mmmm . . . good. Nice and cold." She paused. "Well. I should tell you," she said, "before we actually met, I followed you in the news. I did my research. You are quite the hero, aren't you."

"If you say so," Raymond said, taking a sip of his Dewars and chasing it with the cold club soda. "To me, the only good news is no news." He shot back the rest of his double Dewars and the waitress promptly reappeared, like a magician's assistant, with another one.

"So, I have to tell you, I was interested to learn that your wife was killed on 9/11. Now I can see why you hate these fuckers so bad."

"Yeah, they killed my wife, my nephew, and my cops."

"Was it true that you and Dannis were an item? I heard rumors but wasn't sure, because if you were, why the big secret? You would have been some power couple."

"That's the way we wanted it. Being high profile in this town is bad enough, but then tie in any intimate juicy stuff and they'd be on us 24 hours a day, and we didn't want that, not to mention that the cops, unions, and suspects would have constantly used our relationship as a conflict in just about anything the DA's office was involved in. It was much easier without that perception."

"I'm so sorry," Chernova said. "Horrible what happened to her."

Raymond looked at her, hard. She looked back just as hard.

"So, what's a guy like you do in your time off?" she asked.

"I work, and in my off hours I work out, and I work. That's about it," he said, smiling and feeling a little embarrassed.

"I guess you spent a lot of time with her?"

"As much as we could, but we both had pretty demanding jobs, and our jobs always came first," Raymond said, finishing off his second double. "Sheilah was . . . she was an amazing woman. I believe one day she could have been president of the United States."

"A shame," Chernova said. "I was a big fan of hers." She took another sip, having moved the glass a quarter-turn, leaving another set of red lipstick prints. "How are you doing now? I'm sure you're totally stressed out."

Raymond said nothing. Chernova smiled. "You know what I think? I think you are in major need of some kind of release. I'll bet you're all pent up inside."

"You think so?" Raymond said, and managed a chuckle soaked in sarcasm—what was she getting at?

Chernova came closer. He studied her face. She was a beauty, no doubt about that, he told himself. But this all seemed to be happening so fast—what was she up to?

Without hesitation, she stared deep into his eyes, "So here's what I think we should do. We should continue this conversation at my place, not far from here. We can order in, relax, and talk some more." She scooted out of the seat before Raymond could respond, "Here's the key to my lobby. Let yourself in," she said as she headed for the door.

Raymond wondered what the hell was happening. "Wait, where am I going?"

"Take care of the drinks," she yelled. "And check your text messages."

He looked down at his cell phone, and there was a text: "452 West 44th Street, Apartment 26B XO."

What the fuck, he thought to himself. Was this really happening? He reached into his suit pocket, pulled out his wallet, and called for the check.

His cell phone rang. It was Chernova. He answered, "Yes?"

"I like to be in total control, and just so you know in advance, this applies to everything. Can you take it?"

He felt his inside take an Olympic leap. "What," he stuttered, ". . . what if I say no?"

"You won't! You can't. Get yourself to my apartment, Commissioner."

Raymond laughed softly. "You're a freak," he said, as if he'd just solved an unusually difficult trinomial.

"Congratulations! Now, don't take too long." With that, she hung up.

He threw enough money on the table to cover the check and a generous tip for the waitress.

Ten minutes later he arrived at 26B, and the door was cracked open. He walked into the living room, and the first thing he noticed was the view of the piers and the Jersey skyline on the other side of the Hudson River. Chernova came out of nowhere. "Sit," she said to him, pointing to one of the room's big chairs. He did. "Now, enjoy the show," she said, as she stepped five feet in front of him and unbuttoned her jacket, letting it drop to the floor. She then began undoing her high-collar white ruffled shirt, opening it slowly, never taking her eyes off his until it, too, was gone. His mouth opened slightly, but not as wide as his eyes. Her naked arms and chest were completely covered in beautiful, sensual tattoos. He understood now why she was always so buttoned up. She wiggled out of her skirt. She had on black stockings, garter belt, and nothing else. She kept her high heels on.

She turned around once, slowly, to reveal two full red lips tattooed on each cheek of her bottom. He could see the blue outline of more tattoos that traveled up each of her thighs, but at first, he couldn't make out exactly what they were. Then he did. It was a rattlesnake whose head and fangs began below her belly button and wrapped around her body, its tail resting on her neck just out of sight when she wore her white shirts. There were a dozen more, smaller tats, covering her arms and legs in dark-red and -blue designs. He had never seen anything, or anyone, like her before.

"Where did you get all those tattoos?" he managed to say.

"From my husband."

"Oh." Raymond wasn't sure what that was all about.

"He was very talented. Was. A real artist. Every time he put the needle into me, I would feel a surge. I couldn't get enough of it, or him."

"*Was* a real artist?"

"So you see we have a lot in common. Kenny was a completely beautiful man. He taught me so much about life, about art, about freeing myself to experience real physical and spiritual joy. He died in Afghanistan five years ago. He . . ."

"I'm sorry," Raymond said.

"Don't be. He wouldn't want anyone to feel sorry for him. He lived life up to there," she said, pointing to the ceiling. "Before I met him, I lived down here." She made a leveling gesture with her hand, like a one-armed ump signaling "safe."

"Now you," she said, standing with her hands on her hips. He stood up, took his jacket off. She saw his gun. "Is it loaded, Commissioner?"

"It's always loaded, Mila."

"Miss Chernova. Yes, Miss Chernova."

"Yes, Miss Chernova."

He took off his weapon and laid it on the coffee table, next to her gun and her FBI badge that was in a leather case. He then took his wallet, his shield, and his money clip and put them next to his gun.

He was about to say something when she put one hand behind his head and the fingers of the other on his lips. "Shhh," she said, and proceeded to slowly strip him down and led him over to the bed. "Now, as promised, I'm going to kill you . . ."

He tried not to look shocked.

She smiled. "Kill you with kindness, darling. You really need this . . ."

She put him to bed and he responded like the caged animal he was, growling and snarling to keep up with her.

They didn't stop until almost dawn.

When Raymond finally rolled over, exhausted, Chernova got up—he figured to go to the bathroom. When she returned, he was still half asleep as she slipped one handcuff on him, the other to the vertical brass rod at the head of the bed. "Just to make sure you don't slip away, Commissioner. You see, I'm going to make you confess. I have ways you never dreamed of."

Confess to what, he didn't know. It was going to be a very long morning.

CHAPTER 26

5:15 am, Wednesday, 6 December

Raymond opened his eyes when Chernova pulled open the drapes. The first thing he noticed was the terrible pounding on both sides of his head—he'd only been asleep for two hours, after that Olympian wrestling match. What was she doing already up and about? He went to roll over to his left to get out of bed, when he realized his right arm was still being held up in the air, handcuffed to the brass rod of the bed. Chernova, he could see now, was fully dressed in gym clothes and talking on the phone. When she hung up, she went over to the bed, leaned over, and kissed him good morning on his mouth. She tasted like toothpaste, he thought; not an unpleasant sensation.

"Are you going to take this handcuff off me anytime soon?" Raymond asked.

"Of course, darling. I wouldn't want you to miss your 7 am with the mayor. Wasn't it fun?"

"Fuck! I forgot all about that," he said as she unlocked the cuff on his wrist and his arm dropped. He rubbed it with the fingers of his other hand.

"Listen to me, darling," Chernova said, as she sat on the bed next to him. "No one can know about this. I mean no one. If Jones, especially, finds out, she'll have me in some fucking warehouse counting out confiscated narcotics at JFK." She paused and smiled at him. "We both have a shitload of work to do. I've got to get to the gym, and you should too. We need to build up your stamina."

"Right." Of course she was right. He watched her walk out the door, thinking what the fuck have I done, but after 15 seconds of thinking how bad this was, his thinking dissolved into how good this was, how good she was, and how good he felt. He bounced out of bed and headed for the shower, determined to make the meeting on time.

At 6:15 am, Archer and Shelby picked him up in front of her apartment. They drove quickly, occasionally using the siren, and with seconds to spare, Raymond walked into City Hall on time for the mayor's cabinet meeting.

It went quickly, without incident, and as it broke, the mayor asked Raymond to stay at City Hall for a little longer. "Stop down in my office at eight. Jones from the FBI is coming over to brief me, and I think you should be there. You can grab some breakfast right here."

"Yes sir," he said, and as soon as he was out of sight of the mayor, he called Jones to ask her if there was anything new.

"No," she said, "the mayor's chief of staff called the other day asking for an update, and we scheduled this meeting last night. I called you about nine last night to tell you, but you must have been busy, because you never got back to me."

Raymond felt better that she had called. Although he got along well with Jones and trusted her, he was always leery about her, for reasons he wasn't really aware of. He told her he would meet her in the mayor's office in 15 minutes, and then sat in the outer office, chatting up the secretaries who got in early, as he drained his fourth cup of coffee. Just before eight, Jones cheerfully swung through the door, followed by Chernova. When he saw her, he nearly spit his coffee all over himself. Two hours ago, she had him chained to a fucking bed, and here she was in the office, Miss FBI.

Shelly, the mayor's admin assistant, looked at Raymond and said, "Are we all here?"

"It's just the three of us."

"That's fine. You can all go in. He's waiting for you."

Raymond, Jones, and Chernova entered the mayor's private study. It felt like an icebox in there, Raymond thought to himself. And it stank from the stench of a half-smoked cigar. The two rear windows to the office were opened. "You know it's against the law to smoke in a city building, Mr. Mayor?" Raymond joked.

"I didn't," the mayor responded, "smoke inside. I hung my head out the window, wise ass." Everyone laughed. "Sorry, ladies," he said, looking at Jones and Chernova. Then he got down to business. "So Ms. Jones, what's the latest?"

She stood and recapped what everyone, except the mayor, already knew, that the Bureau and the police were confident Samadi was the cell team leader from Detroit, and was now in New York City, but that they had not exactly located him yet. They were aware he had six or seven others on the ground here as well, but they, too, were not ID'd or pinpointed. She explained how the Bureau found them by encouraging Hamadi to give them up, and how the cell was using sophisticated technology and cryptic codes to circumvent detection, and how the people at the Bureau were confident they would break the cell.

A silence fell on the room and hung like a low cloud. The mayor, who had relit his cigar, now carefully rested it on the edge of his ashtray, intending to let it go out. He stood up, with panic in his eyes.

"Great work, people." He paused, went to the fireplace, put one hand up on the mantel, then turned around, his tone conciliatory.

"Look, I can't afford another attack on the city during this election year," and no sooner than those words had come out of his mouth, he realized how he sounded, and he tried to clean it up. "Look," he said, "no one wants any bloodshed in this city, and not just because of the election, of course. I don't want you people to think I only give a fuck about getting reelected."

Still in his seat, Raymond said, softly and evenly, "Mr. Mayor, we're doing everything in our power to make sure we get to them before they get to us."

"We're on it," Jones said, as reassuringly she could make it sound, as she and Chernova stood, sensing the meeting was over. Raymond stood as well.

"Thanks, people," Brown said. "Keep me updated."

Raymond, Jones, and Chernova left the mayor's office, walked down the large tomb-like granite hallway, and, as soon as they cleared the security checkpoint, Chernova said, under her breath, "I hate fucking politicians. Reelect me, even if there's no one left alive for me to govern." Jones and Chernova got in Jones's car and headed back to FBI headquarters, and Raymond got in his car for the five-minute drive to One Police Plaza.

Once he was up in the office, he called Chernova to ask if she wanted to stay with him that night in Midtown, but he didn't feel a good vibe back, and wasn't sure why. Maybe she forgot her handcuffs. Maybe she was having her period. Maybe he was having his. Maybe she felt sorry for Hamadi, or, of all things, maybe she actually felt sorry for him. "Next time," he said and hung up.

He needed to put her out of his head for now, and started shuffling papers on his desk, trying to find his daily schedule. He called in Gallagher and rattled off the names of five different chiefs and four deputy commissioners he wanted to see. Then he began bitching about the unions and the press, and just as he did, his cell phone rang. His stomach knotted. It was Breshill.

"What's up?" he said as he answered it.

"Commissioner! How's it going? Anything new? I heard you guys went over to see Hamadi. Anything?"

"How the fuck do you know we went to see Hamadi?"

"Commissioner, the assistant director of the New York FBI office, the New York City police commissioner, and the hottest FBI agent in the country walk into MCC, and you don't think my phone wasn't ringing off the hook?"

"I can't get into it right now."

"I'm not asking, but if something comes up, I trust you'll keep me in mind."

"I'll do that." As soon as Raymond hung up, he started giving Gallagher more assignments. At one point, he jumped up and said, "I've got to go get my shoes shined."

Gallagher looked at him for a minute and then said, "Okay, what's up? Did you drink a pot of espresso or have you been eating a bunch of those chocolate coins from Peter Luger's?

"What?"

"Don't *what* me. You haven't had this much energy in weeks, and all of a sudden, it's like somebody stuck a jet fuel pipe up your ass."

Raymond stood there for a second, broke into a smile. Gallagher winced.

"Oh no. what? What did you do?"

"I haven't done anything."

"Commissioner . . ."

"Jerry, I haven't done anything you need to know about. Now leave me the fuck alone." Raymond couldn't help chuckle as he walked out the door of his office and headed to the elevator, with Archer, as always, in tow. "Jon, let's go get a shine!"

CHAPTER 27

9:57 am, Thursday, 7 December

I t was on.

With all the wiretaps approved by the Justice Department and a federal judge, Agent Jones, operating out of her private office on the 28th floor, designated an entire section of the FBI's 26th floor Tech Room as the plant—the wire room—for this investigation. They were up now on eight different cell phones by the authority of the FISA court that gave them the legal authority to follow the voice. If the caller told the person he was speaking with to call him at another number, the Feds would be able to hit a switch and get up on that phone without having to go through a three-day warrant approval process.

Phones were normally monitored from 8 am to midnight, unless special circumstances led the authorities to believe the callers might engage in criminal activity outside those hours. Because of that, Jones expanded the plant's operation to run 24 hours a day, in the event that Samadi and his goons jumped on their phones in the middle of the night. Two dozen civilian translators, eight FBI agents and cops, and a few supervisors were assigned to the plant, and another eighteen JTTF members were put on as stand-by surveillance teams if these guys could be identified.

Chernova was there as well, along with a number of other agents assigned as support staff, tasked with gathering intelligence and following up on any leads. Raymond was attending a community breakfast in the 79th Precinct, in Bedford-Stuyvesant, Brooklyn.

At 9:57, a call came in to Samadi. The plant hushed as the translator switched on his speaker key to allow a portion of the room to hear the Arabic conversation. As the voice spoke, it was immediately translated into English and posted on all the plant's screens: "The chariot is ready, and with it, the lightning bolts will come from the eyes of Allah to strike down the infidels."

There was a pause, and then Samadi's voice responded: "Good, my son. Stay prepared and stay ready. The time is coming soon when Allah will call you to him."

Chernova was sending the translated text to both Jones and Raymond. Several of the translators began speaking in Arabic, and one of the supervisors grabbed Chernova's arm and pulled her close. He whispered in her ear: "That's the voice of the man who decapitated the district attorney." He knew what he was talking about. They had listened to those voices on the video made in Dannis's apartment a hundred times already.

Chernova felt nauseous as she continued to study the screens, typing into her phone without even looking. She sent a separate text to Raymond: "The caller is one of the men that killed Sheilah." A chill went through him as he read it.

Another call came a few minutes later: "In the name of Allah the Merciful. My brothers and I need two more days. We have eyes on the insects, hundreds of them all in one place at the same time. It will be a glorious victory and Allah will reward us greatly. Stay safe, my brother. As-Salaam-Alaikum."

"As-Salaam-Alaikum." The line went dead.

And another call: "My brothers have been walking between the parking garage and the money factory." Then the line went dead.

Ten minutes after, Jones stormed into the plant, followed by two suits, and huddled with Chernova in a cubicle. On a big screen in the middle of the room, the typewritten translation of this latest exchange began appearing, and next to each line, in red, question marks appeared next to words. The chariot? The insects? Hundreds of them? The parking garage? The money factory?

"What the hell are they talking about?" Jones said to Chernova, but before she could answer, her cell phone rang. It was Raymond.

"I'm here with Jones," she said. "I'm putting you on speaker."

"Hey guys," Raymond said, his voice crackling and amplified. "I'm just leaving Brooklyn. How's it going?"

Chernova answered, "We're waiting for our guys to tell us what cell sites these calls were coming from, and then we'll have a better idea what they're talking about."

"I'm free after four o'clock. I'll stop by," Raymond said.

"See you then," Chernova said and disconnected.

As Jones and Chernova continued to stare at the wall monitors, Chernova started speaking, analyzing out loud.

"The chariot could be some kind of large vehicle they're planning to use, like they did in Nice, London, and Barcelona. It's right out of the ISIS playbook. Insects are probably people, hundreds of them, maybe Rock Center again . . money factory could be a bank." She paused and looked directly at Jones. "The insects—that call is coming from the Upper East Side, diagonally across from a Jewish day school, where children ages six through fourteen attend. Two or three hundred kids every day."

"The money factory?" Jones asked.

"Maybe the New York Stock Exchange. That phone is pinging off a cell tower at Water Street and Wall. It's got to be a bank, or the stock exchange itself. These could be the two targets, the school and the stock exchange. The chariot—I don't know yet. Maybe a vehicle with explosives."

Jones nodded. "Good work, Mila." She then turned to the people in the room and called them to attention. "Listen up, everyone. We are going on high alert to track these killers. It's going to be impossible to rely just on their phones, because they don't use them often enough. You will scour all local mosques, and wherever Arabs hang out in the city. And get your sources out there. Don't tell them what we're looking for; just let them know we'll pay well for good information. Find out if there are any new members who may have joined in the last few weeks. Let's get on it, people. *Let's get on it!*"

CHAPTER 28

5:55 pm, Friday, 8 December

At dawn, every available member of the joint FBI and the NYPD terrorism task force in New York and New Jersey were put on high alert, to look for who Raymond and Jones now believed were eight terrorists and their Detroit-based leader, Samadi. All available intelligence assets were put on active duty and assigned to work in teams. Throughout the day, they were sent to scour local mosques and known Arab hangouts, running checks on imams, and the like. After an exhaustive number of searches, they were unable to turn up anything that might lead them to the attackers.

It wasn't until shortly after five that afternoon that the FBI command center at Federal Plaza picked up a single new call to Samadi's cell phone, just the kind of

slip-up they were hoping for. Within minutes, Mila had the translation up on her screen, with Jones and Raymond huddled behind her:
"You will see our chariot at the end of the block by the red house and
chocolate factory. We are up the street."

"Where?" Jones asked.

"I can't tell yet," Chernova said.

"Get on AT&T," Jones told her tech specialists, who were able
to locate the source of the call inside a relatively small perimeter in
the vicinity of Houston and Church Streets. Jones immediately dispatched two surveillance teams to the area, looking for anything that
could be linked in any way to the color red and chocolate.

An hour later, one of the agents noticed a candy store on
MacDougal and Houston and a firehouse nearby on Church. He
relayed what he found to Jones, who asked if any of the teams saw
anything nearby those possibles that could be defined as a chariot.
Two of the Feds in one of the surveillance teams, of Arab descent,
got out of their vehicle and walked along Houston, pretending to be
deep in a spirited discussion about the New York Yankees. Houston,
a main thoroughfare, had several bars that catered to nearby NYU
students and the SoHo crowd. The agents stopped in each, continuing to talk as they looked around, alternating going to the men's
room. They came up with nothing. As they were leaving the last bar,
a young Irish waitress came over and asked if she could help them.
One of the agents, Azi, smiled and said, "We were supposed to meet
a bunch of guys here. Did anyone ask for Azi?"

"I think you just missed them," the waitress said, smiling. "They
left about 20 minutes ago. Eight guys, right?"

The two agents looked at each other quickly; then Azi said, "Yes,
thanks. We'll catch them on their cells. Meanwhile, let's have a beer,
okay?"

"Sure thing," she chirped, as they sat on two stools at one end of
the bar. The bartender, a burly Irish fellow whose apron came up to
just under his armpits, bounced the two draughts on the bar, and,

in the same motion, slid over a wooden bowl of pretzels. When the waitress walked by again, Azi lifted his mug and said, "Cheers."

Before she could move on, he asked her if she had ever seen his friends come in before. "Nope, never seen them. I've been here for five years now, and I have to say I'm pretty good with faces." Azi smiled, took another sip of his beer, and his partner took one off his. Azi dropped a few bills on the bar and they left. Once inside the car, Azi got on the horn and called Jones at the command center.

"We have a confirmed spot," Azi said, and he gave the name and address of the bar. "They have electronic surveillance in the bar. There are additional businesses on the street that also have cameras. There is also a UPS parking lot on Church and Hudson that must have dozens of cameras."

"Good work," Jones said, and called out to one of her legal team to start working up warrants for every camera on the street.

"Hold on," Azi said. "I think I can get the bar's camera without a warrant. Give me 15 minutes."

"Do it," Jones said.

Azi and his partner went back to the pub and waved the waitress over. Then Azi pulled out his FBI ID. He explained to her that he and his partner were with the Justice Department. She looked at him quizzically, feeling a bit taken aback and confused about why they hadn't said they were with the Bureau from the beginning. "Those cameras you have," he said, pointing to the ceiling. "Are they active?"

"Yes sir. Why? Those guys you were looking for when you came in, they were speaking what sounded like Arabic. That's why you were looking for them, right?"

"Right," Azi said.

"Come on," she said as she took the two agents to the back, where a door opened to a set of stairs that led to the basement and a private office. She knocked on the office door, and a middle-aged woman opened it. "What is it, Lylah?"

"These men are from the FBI."

The woman eyed them suspiciously and asked for their IDs. After she carefully looked at each, she said, "So, what do you want?"

"We'd like to have a copy of your security camera recordings from today."

"I guess it's all right," she said, and Azi handed her a flash drive. Thirty seconds later, he had the entire day downloaded on it.

"Thanks," Azi said. Lylah led the two agents back up the stairs and to the front entrance.

"Come back sometime," she said to Azi, with a grin on her face. He waved goodbye, and the two agents got back into their car and called Jones.

"We got it," Azi said. "I'll send it to you right now." He jumped out of the car, opened the trunk, and pulled out a black hard-plastic briefcase. He sat back in the car, opened the case that contained a computer. He turned it on, put the drive into the computer, and clicked it on to Jones's dedicated line. Five minutes later, every member of surveillance had stills of all eight men on their computer screens and their iPhones.

Just before 8:30 pm, FBI agents Jones and Chernova pulled into the underground garage at One Police Plaza. Archer was there to meet them and bring them up to the commissioner's office. Their private elevator stopped on the 14th floor, and Joe Allegra, the chief of department, greeted them. He tried his best not to stare at Chernova, but it wasn't easy; her beauty was enhanced by the overpowering Chanel perfume. Jones, Chernova, and Allegra walked to the commissioner's office together, where Gallagher met them and waved them in. "He's waiting for you," he said.

As the three entered the office, Gallagher took the coffee orders, "Coffee, latte, or espresso?" he asked.

"Latte?" Jones said, smiling.

"Yeah, he's got a fucking combination Starbucks and cigar bar in his office, and I'm not sure what else. I'm afraid to go in there sometimes," Raymond said, and they all laughed. When the lattes arrived, Raymond began, "Tell me what you know. I've got to be at

Gracie Mansion tonight at ten o'clock to brief the mayor. I also want the chief here to be brought up to speed."

"No problem," Jones said. "I think we're getting there. We're going to be set up early tomorrow with extra surveillance teams. As soon as they phone in the morning, we're going to try to be on top of the areas they're calling from to see if we can find them. Mila thinks she has some of it figured out, but we're still missing some of the pieces."

Chernova added: "What we know for sure is that their target locations appear to be a Jewish day school on the Upper East Side and a destination somewhere near Wall Street, either the stock exchange or a bank. The cell leader, Samadi, is working with six or seven more players. According to the interpreters on the wire, one is definitely the terrorist who killed Dannis."

Raymond then told Allegra to put together a plainclothes detail to saturate those two areas. He didn't want to wait for any more information. "Maybe our guys will see something before these assholes make their move." He thanked Jones and Chernova, and said, "Okay, I've got to get to the Mansion to see the mayor, and then I'm heading home because Jerry and I are driving up to Albany for breakfast with the governor. I'll call you guys in the morning as soon as I'm done in Albany."

Just after 11 pm, Archer escorted Raymond to the front door of his building, opened the door, and walked in behind him. Out of the corner of his eye, he saw someone who had been sitting on a couch in the lobby stand up. "Good evening, Jonathan," Chernova said, smiling as she walked toward them.

Archer looked at his boss and back at her. "Good evening ma'am."

"How'd you get in here?" Raymond asked, feeling a little uncomfortable in front of Archer.

"I've got my ways," she said.

As the three of them walked to the elevator, Raymond looked at Archer and said, "I'm good; go ahead. I'll see you in the morning."

Then Chernova chimed in, "Yes Jon. I'll take good care of him from here."

Archer stopped dead in his tracks and smiled as the two entered the elevator. "Yes ma'am. I'm sure you will."

Chernova followed Raymond into his apartment, and the second the door closed, he pushed her against the wall and kissed her deeply, then left her standing there and walked into the bathroom and closed the door. When he walked out, he found Chernova sitting in a big, cushiony chair, smiling, nude, her tattoos glistening as though they were alive, her dark hair down to her shoulders. "Hello, Commissioner! What a surprise to see you here."

He smiled. "No, it's a surprise to see you here, Mila, considering it's my apartment. How did you get in downstairs?"

"I work for the FBI; I have ways." They both laughed, as he began peeling out of his clothes at the speed of sound. "Nice," she said, her eyes looking down at him.

"I'll take a shower."

"I'll be waiting in bed. Don't be too long. Understand?"

Raymond nodded. He turned to the bathroom, then turned his head back. "With handcuffs or without?" She laughed.

They made love until they were both sweaty and exhausted. Raymond put his head back on the pillow. He was coming back to life, he thought to himself. "Thank you," he said.

"For what? I'm not a charity, you know."

"I know. I just . . . you're a gift to me. I don't know how else to say it."

"Then don't say anything," Mila said. After a few minutes, she sat up in bed. "Rick, I have something I want to tell you."

"What is it?"

"Listen carefully to me. On my way here, I had a call from an agent at the plant. They're going back through all the text messages that were found on what we believe to be Samadi's old phone, right after Jimmy and our agents were killed in Fayetteville. They think they found something. Jones will call you in the morning to tell you, so act surprised. They found a text mentioning you by name."

Raymond's eyes widened. "Me, personally?"

"Yes. Samadi singled you out for a jihad; he wants to do to you what he did to Sheilah."

Raymond paused and pressed his lips together. "I'm sure."

"The text said something like, 'It's personal' . . . and to bring him your head."

"I'm going to kill this fucker. And then I'm going to get every one of his goons."

Chernova put her arms around him. "I will be right there with you, every step of the way." She paused, kissed him, then said, "Please be careful. You are Samadi's prize. Your death would be his greatest victory."

They came together for the rest of the night, partners in love and partners in murder and death.

CHAPTER 29

5:00 pm, Saturday, 9 December

A t five that afternoon, three calls to Samadi's
line were picked up at the FBI command center. All of them ended with the caller praying
for success *in the coming day* against the hundreds of
insects, praising Allah, and praying they would see
Samadi in heaven. The Bureau was certain now the
attack was to be on the Jewish day school; nothing else
in that area matched for a target. It was set for 1 pm on
Monday the 13th.

Chernova had the locations of two of thethe callers in less than a minute, one was calling from the
vicinity of 67th and Park Avenue, and the other one
was down around Wall Street and Broadway. "They're
going to hit the school; that's the 'hundred insects,' and
something down around Wall Street at the same time."

Jones ordered a surveillance van and four unmarked cars into the area of Park and 67th to try to locate the callers, and the same for the area around Broadway and Wall Street, but both attempts failed. One tech van in each location was disguised as a Con Ed truck. The vehicles roamed the streets with a fishnet machine, something that could immediately pick up electronic serial numbers from close-by phones. The Feds had the phone numbers that the terrorists were using, and hoped the fishnet would locate them, but the callers had immediately shut their phones down after they made the calls, eliminating any chance of capturing the electronic serial numbers on their phones which would have pinpointed their axact locations.

Jones and Raymond called for a joint meeting of the entire team at FBI headquarters for eight that night. Jones also called in their best hostage negotiation team from Washington, D.C., and asked Raymond to alert the NYPD counterterrorism team leaders, as well as the commander of the emergency service unit, and ask them to attend the meeting.

In the conference room, Jones stood at the head of the table and laid out her plan. "We're going to have 100 cops in Downtown Manhattan, to build a perimeter around Wall Street, half in uniform, the other half in plainclothes." NYPD had already stopped two dozen vans in Lower Manhattan and had turned up nothing. Raymond ordered a counterassault team immediately to be placed inside the perimeter of the New York Stock Exchange, and to have the NYPD technical assistance unit work with the FBI. Jones ordered an FBI sniper and assault team to immediately gain entrance to the school, while the technical unit installed cameras in every hallway, at every door.

Raymond took over. "We have decided not to close the school on Monday. We're still not sure what the terrorists' plan is, but don't want to alert them by shutting it down. As soon as the kids arrive, they will be brought to one of the two large gyms in the basement that were originally built with the highest sense of security for everyday use, and specifically for this kind of attack."

The meeting adjourned, and Raymond asked Gallagher and Chernova to come back to Police Plaza with him. On the way over, in the Suburban, with Chernova next to him in the back seat, Raymond asked her again if she was convinced that Samadi was one of the eight men they'd singled out. "I can't be 100 percent sure," she said, "but I don't think he would want to miss out on the action. There is one thing I would consider, Commissioner."

"And that is?"

"He's an egomaniac. I'm not sure he's as willing to die for Allah as the others. None of them believe the bullshit they talk to their underlings as they march them willingly to their death. Bin Laden hid in a compound for five years, Sadam Hussein in a spider hole, as well as Qadafi. They're all about jihad as long as someone else is doing the fighting, and the dying."

Raymond sat back and blew out a stream of air, his eyes fixed on the roof of the car. "He's the one who killed Sheilah?"

"No doubt. The voice biometrics from the video in her apartment and the one from the calls are a perfect match.

Raymond turned to her. "I want Samadi," he said softly.

"As much as he wants you," she said.

He leaned forward and said to Gallagher, "I'm going to hang out in the office tomorrow; if you're not doing anything, come see me."

He turned to Chernova. "Where can I drop you?"

"My apartment."

Raymond instructed Shelby to drop him and Gallagher at One Police Plaza and then to take Chernova to her apartment. They got out of the car, and Raymond nodded to Chernova and watched Shelby drive off.

"Staying?" he said to Gallagher, who nodded, no, "I'll be back nice and early."

Raymond looked at his watch. "I'm going to stay in the office tonight. Tell Shelby to be here around 9 am."

"Yes sir," Gallagher walked toward his car, and Archer and Raymond walked toward the elevator.

The next morning Raymond was up early, went down to the gym on the eighth floor, and worked out for an hour, then spent 30 minutes on the treadmill. Then he went back up to his office and shuffled paper for the rest of the morning. Right around lunchtime as he got to the bottom of his in-box, he found a fat envelope from the attorney he retained to review Sheilah's will. He opened the envelope and found a letter and about a three-fourth-inch stack of legal documents, some of the pages with yellow tabs attached. He read the letter and first few documents, and broke down in tears. Sheilah Dannis had left him over $30 million. His heart raced as he read each page that he had to sign, which included the opening of bank and investment accounts to where the money would be transferred. Most of what he was reading, he didn't even understand. By the time he was finished, he was exhausted and drained.

Gallagher showed up, and they went to lunch and discussed the financial implications of Dannis's will and trust. "Should I resign? Should I tell the mayor? What happens when the press finds out?"

"Fuck everybody," Gallagher said. "It's no one's business. As for you retiring? Sure, go home, sit around, and do nothing. In two fucking weeks you'll be calling me looking for a job. Stop the bullshit. You're not going anywhere! Take the afternoon off and relax. We've got a big day tomorrow."

Monday morning, Raymond was up by five, took a shower, changed his clothes, and told Gallagher to meet him at headquarters by six. They were driven to a temporary command center positioned on the Upper East Side, and verified that 100 police officers, both in and out of uniform, had saturated the Financial District. Members of the NYPD ESU and FBI counterassault team were inside the stock exchange, and marked and unmarked cars were spread out over five locations around a loose perimeter, loaded with ESU officers armed with heavy weapons.

From the command center, Raymond and his counterterrorist commanders, Jones, Chernova and a number of FBI agents, and Gallagher studied the security cameras as the children filed into school and their parents departed. Hostage negotiation and counter-assault teams had entered the school at 3 am, and were now staked out on the upper floors, hidden from sight; they placed additional security cameras and were ready to strike or deal, whichever opportunity presented itself.

The team at the command center was also monitoring the cameras covering Wall Street when a surveillance team on Canal Street spotted a large black Mercedes Sprinter van just like the one they had seen in the West Village near the UPS parking lot coming over the Brooklyn Bridge. Once the van reached the Manhattan side of the bridge, it jumped on to the FDR Drive northbound, and away from the Financial District. The NYPD/FBI surveillance team that was now on the van was convinced that either this wasn't the van, or perhaps it was heading to the Jewish day school on the Upper East Side. However, when it reached Grand Street, it got off at the exit and headed west. Just as the surveillance cars were ready to break off the tail, the Sprinter made a U-turn and headed back to the FDR Drive, this time going south. The driver came off the drive, heading right toward the NYPD temporary headquarters vehicle, and at the corner of Water Street, made a left, going back toward Wall Street. At this point, everyone's senses were jumping, after believing that they were on the wrong track.

"He's not going to get into Wall Street," the ESU commander radioed back. "They won't be able to get through those barriers we dropped at Water and Wall."

As the van approached the corner of Wall, it slowed down just a bit, continuing to travel south. The surveillance car radioed, "He didn't attempt to pull into the block." After a full minute of silence, the radio came back on: "Surveillance 6 to ESU 2, the vehicle just made a U-turn and is heading north again on Water, and he seems to be picking up speed. He's making a left on Maiden Lane"; that was two blocks north of Wall Street. "He's making a left on Pearl, heading back to Wall."

"Stop him at Pine Street. Don't let him get to Wall," the ESU commander yelled. "Stop him now."

An unmarked surveillance car pulled in at the corner of Pine and Pearl Streets to cut off the van's access to Wall Street, one block away. As the car did, the van sped up and crashed into it, pushing the car to the side, passing it. The surveillance car hit its siren, and the driver screamed into the radio, "It's going down. They're going to get to the barricades at Wall and Pearl!"

When the van got there, it was stopped by the concrete barricades. Three men jumped out of the van and began running toward the stock exchange. From two unmarked emergency services vehicles just off Water, eight SWAT-dressed cops jumped out and began running to where the van had stopped. Two of the cops stopped there; the others kept running, just behind the three terrorists.

The ESU team commander yelled over the radio for all units to back away from the van as the team approached. The team's M4 machine guns were at the ready, as the officers knelt behind the massive concrete barricades, yelling at passersby on the street to clear the area, while aiming at the driver, who was sitting and staring ahead without moving.

Seconds passed until, suddenly, the driver of the van yelled, "*Allahu Akbar.*" The van exploded, blowing the unmarked surveillance car behind it into a million bits. The fronts of the buildings on Pearl and Wall that took the brunt of the blast were peeled off the buildings, and every window was shattered. The cops behind the barricades could feel debris scour their skin, saved only by the barrier.

At the same time, the three terrorists from the van ran toward the stock exchange, each carrying a large canvas duffel bag. Suddenly, they stopped, pulled out AK-47s from the bags, and started running toward the entrance of the exchange.

They never made it in.

"*Down,*" a SWAT officer yelled, and any civilians who had not already run when the van exploded fell flat on the ground, as the terrorists got to one knee. None was able to get a single shot off, as they were surrounded by CAT and SWAT teams who mowed them down. They never knew what hit them. One terrorist, wounded but not dead, slowly got up.

"Kill him . . . *Kill him now!*" an FBI supervisor on the scene screamed as one of the SWAT team members, with a spray of automatic rifle fire, cut the terrorist in half.

At the same time, the surveillance teams on the Upper East Side I.D.'d two cars they believed were headed for the school, each with two occupants. "Fuck," Raymond yelled, as he watched the camera feed. The two cars blocked off 67th Street at Park and at Lexington, cutting off access to the street from both sides. Two men leapt from each of the two cars, all the men armed with automatic rifles and wearing bomb vests, and ran for the front entrance of the school. Don't let them get into that school, Raymond thought to himself, just before the terrorists' two cars exploded, sounding like an earthquake and looking like fireworks on the Fourth of July. Debris was flying everywhere.

The terrorists sprinted toward the school entrance, then opened fire on the guard in front of the school, who managed to get back inside, leaving the entrance doors open as he did. Sirens could be heard as fire trucks and police cars headed for the scene, along with the CAT and SWAT teams that had been watching the entrance to the school. The terrorists ran in through the front doors and went from classroom to classroom, confused and angered that they couldn't find any students or teachers to kill. They headed for the stairwell, and as they entered, two FBI agents on the next landing hurled two stun grenades at their feet; the blast sounded like a massive explosion. It knocked the terrorists back on their rears, their legs flying up in front of them, and they were completely dazed. Just as they tried to compose themselves and regroup, a dozen FBI agents and ESU cops came flying down the stairs; they killed all four before they could pick up their weapons again. The agents then headed outside to make sure there were no others trying to get in.

There weren't. It was over.

Not long after, Raymond and Jones received official word—dozens of civilians were hurt by the two explosions downtown, none critical, there was plenty of property damage, but the only casualties were the eight terrorists. Not a single NYPD member or federal agent was taken down.

CHAPTER 30

6:00 pm, Monday, 11 December

The news of the attack was relayed instantly around the world. TV crews were dispatched to both sites of attack, but could not get close because of police yellow tape. They also converged on City Hall, where a press conference was scheduled for six o'clock, perfectly timed to make the national nightly news broadcasts in the States, and then endlessly replayed on every available outlet. Dozens of reporters from CNN, Fox, MSNBC, the three major networks, Al Jazeera, the BBC, Agence France-Presse, the China Daily, and at least 50 other agencies swarmed the city.

In Raymond's office, he, Chernova, Gallagher, and Jones were having coffee. "One more battle in a never-ending war," Jones said. "We won this time, but who knows what will happen tomorrow."

"We'll be ready for them," Raymond said. "And let's not forget Agent Chernova. Without her help, who knows where we would be.

"Absolutely," Jones said. "It's an electronic war as much as it is a weapons one. Mila is a warrior. I'm glad she's on our side.

"Me too," Raymond said, unable to stifle a laugh. So," he continued, "do you think we got Samadi? Are the IDs done yet?"

"Hard to tell for sure. The bodies of the terrorists with the bombs were blown to bits. I doubt he was one of those shot down in front of Wall Street."

"But your best guess is he's dead?"

"Yes, for what it's worth. Would he send his own men out and miss the glory of his big day? I doubt it."

"He might," Raymond said. "You know, they promise these guys a catered affair at the world's greatest strip club when they go to heaven. Most of them can't wait, because the only sex they've ever had is if they were in a rape squad."

"Poor demented fucks," Mila said.

"Yeah, but I'm not convinced until forensics confirms eight bodies that he's dead. He's a slippery little snake who doesn't mind killing his own men but cries when he cuts himself shaving."

"I wouldn't worry about it," Jones said. "Where is he going to hide now? The whole world knows what happened. Every fuckin' bad guy in the city will be looking over his shoulder, and any of them aligned with ISIS will be looking to get out any way they can."

"Until the next time," Raymond said.

"Until the next time. We'll be ready." Jones looked at her watch. "I think it's time we head over to City Hall."

"Yeah," Raymond said, and nodded to Gallagher, who called down to Shelby to have the Suburban ready. Outside the plaza, fully armed police had ringed the front entrance. Nobody was taking any chances. "Welcome to today's America," Raymond muttered.

They piled into the Suburban for the short drive over to City Hall.

A crowd of reporters, cameras, and microphones filled the Blue Room of City Hall. Every nearby sidewalk was parked full of satellite vans, ringed with security. A half-dozen microphones were set up at the mayor's podium, waiting for him to make his appearance. Shelby hit the emergency lights on the Suburban as he approached the huge metal barriers that were sticking out of the ground, and they were lowered into the ground as he came to the driveway. He pulled right up to the outside steps of City Hall while the two backup vehicles, one belonging to Jones and the FBI, parked and idled on the far side of the plaza. Raymond, Jones, Gallagher, and Chernova got out of the Suburban, walked up the stairs, and turned toward the mayor's office, with a detective from the Intelligence Division holding open a thick metal gate as they approached.

They went to the mayor's waiting area, from where they could see the packed Blue Room filled with reporters pushing each other out of the way to get the best camera position.

The mayor walked out of his office to the waiting area, shook their hands, and said, "Congratulations!"

"Thank you, Mr. Mayor," Jones said.

Raymond said, "Yes, thank you. It really wasn't us, as much as it was the men and women that work for us, Mila and Jerry here among them. The FBI's SWAT team and our ESU were superb."

"Rick, that's exactly what I wanted to talk to you about. I was going to have a bunch of them down here for this presser, but there are too many, and we didn't have a lot of time to prepare."

There was a knock on the door, signaling that it was time to go. "I'm going to wait right here," Chernova said. As the primary case agent, she was most valuable if she had no face to show to the enemy.

One by one the others filed into the Blue Room as the mayor's press secretary yelled, "Heads up!" a signal that they were about to get started.

Outside, between the Blue Room and the mayor's office, a dozen police, in suits, scoured the hallways, waiting for the mayor to conclude and return to his office. Just inside the mayor's waiting room, barely visible, were three uniformed ESU cops, standing at the ready with M4 automatic weapons, looking like they were heading to Baghdad.

As the mayor centered himself on the podium, the others positioned themselves on his right and left. There was a blinding burst of electronic lights from the photographers. Others behind them shouted for them to kneel so they could get their shot. When the flashing ended, the mayor began to speak: "This is, indeed, a great day for the city of New York. Buildings can be rebuilt; streets can be repaired; our injured can heal. What will never happen is that these scum that tried to take down our wonderful city will ever have that chance again." A small group of the mayor's staff and supporters in the back of the room cheered; some of the uniformed and plain-clothes cops applauded.

"Before I go any further, I want to introduce to you two of the heroes who helped to thwart this attack. FBI Deputy Director Chelsea Jones, would you please say a few words?"

Jones nodded, and, by habit, scanned the crowd as she spoke. "Thank you, Mr. Mayor. As the saying goes, we were all just doing our jobs. I stand here today before you, but I represent hundreds of FBI agents and personnel who have been on this case for months. Our job is to protect the citizens of this great country, and our great city. Thank you."

"Commissioner Raymond . . . Rick, get up here," the mayor said, waving him to the microphones. As Raymond stepped up to the podium, he thought about what he should say. Should he talk about Sheilah? Jimmy?

"Thank you, Mr. Mayor. I can't say enough good things about Agent Jones and the incredible team of police and FBI agents who wiped out this evil bunch—and make no mistake, these terrorists aren't political warriors; they are cold-blooded killers, without morals, without values, without anything but the lust for killing those of us who believe in freedom." Not bad, he thought, as he noticed most of the reporters in the room nodding and some smiling.

"We have paid a great price for this day. For me, this day was a very personal one. As most of you know, the enemy, these demented and evil people that have hijacked the Koran and are the outlaws of

Islam, were responsible for killing my cops, killing my nephew, and killing my wife, Mary, on September 11, 2001. After I lost my wife, I never thought I'd love again, but I did." Then what he said next stunned the group of reporters, but not more than the mayor and Jones. "I loved Sheilah Dannis with all my heart. She was young, brilliant, with a career that had no bounds in the years ahead. She was the best of us, and when she died, a little bit of every free man and woman died with her. I have promised her family, and my sister Linda, Jimmy's mom, and the families of those cops that we have lost, that their deaths would not be in vain. That I will continue to take the fight to the enemy, and as long as I am in command of the NYPD, I will do everything in my power to exterminate this evil. And that's what I intend to do. Thank you, and God bless America."

And that said it all.

Raymond stepped back to a round of polite applause. No one was quite sure what he was talking about, or how close he really was to the DA, but he didn't care anymore. He had done his job, and that's all that mattered to him now.

The mayor took over the microphones again. "Thank you, everybody, and we're going to hold off on taking any questions for now. We'll reconvene tomorrow and you can ask away. Thank you again!"

The four walked out of the Blue Room and back into the mayor's waiting room, where Jones, Gallagher, and Raymond rejoined Chernova. "Let's go," Jones said.

As everyone was about to leave, the mayor called Raymond into his office, and when they were alone, Brown said, "Are you okay, Rick? Is everything okay?"

"Yes sir, fine . . . I'm fine, just fine." He left the office and met Gallagher outside by the Suburban. Gallagher jumped in the back seat of the SUV with Raymond, and neither said a word to the other. "Back to the office," Gallagher said to Shelby and Archer.

CHAPTER 31

7:00 am, Tuesday, 12 December

Raymond opened his eyes at seven, later than he usually awakened. He pulled one of the four pillows on the bed close and embraced it like it was a woman, as he thought about Sheilah. It was the first time he stayed at the Marcus since her death, and returning to their suite was harder than he anticipated. The general manager had met him the night before when he arrived to get him situated, knowing he was now actually one of the hotel's principal owners. As the general manager was leaving Raymond's suite, he stopped at the door and looked back in and said, "I saw your press conference yesterday. I was proud of you and I was proud of her," and then he walked out and closed the door behind him.

Raymond stayed in bed that way for a long time, as the flash cards of their days flipped through his mind's eye. It was after eight before he finally pulled back the quilt, went to the bathroom, took a shower, and shaved. Next he went to the door and found his clothes, which had been picked up during the night, now cleaned, pressed, and delivered in a box and on hangers on a luggage rack. His black shoes had been mirror-shined.

Before he dressed, he ordered up some breakfast—three eggs, bacon, sausage, coffee, chilled orange-grapefruit juice. It came on a cart in 20 minutes, delivered and set up for him by one of the VIP butlers. He ate on a small table, while still in his robe, trying to figure out which of the miniature square bottles was the salt and which was the pepper, before using both in equal measure. As he ate, he watched TV with the sound off, clicking around the news networks like an erratic cowbell player in a small-club Latin band. He went back and forth between CNN and Fox, then jumped to MSNBC, losing CNN in the remote pattern, and finally going over to the all-Spanish news station provided by the hotel. With no sound, it didn't make any difference. The footage Jones had given the networks was impressive, he thought to himself; it showed the actual attack from the point of view of the dozens of security cameras—New York's finest and the FBI's elite doing combat on the streets of the city he loved.

After an hour or so of seeing the same footage over and over, and pictures of the mayor preening in the Blue Room, he used the remote to shut off the set. He picked up the newspaper and saw the latest headline of the *New York Herald*:

HERO COPS AND COMMISSIONER
WORK WITH FBI TO BATTLE TERRORISTS
Story by Sammy Breshill starts on page 3

He wondered who Breshill was able to reach. He didn't read the piece; there was nothing the reporter could tell him he didn't know.

His phone buzzed on the night table. He had been avoiding checking his messages. He was sure there were a lot of reporters trying to bang him. He ran down the call list and stopped when he saw Linda's name. He hit the call-back, and she picked up on the second ring. "Linda," he said,. "How are you?"

"Fine," she said. "I've been watching the news and just wanted to make sure that you're okay."

"I am. In some strange way, I feel good that we did what we did, but it never takes away the pain of the loss. I know you know what I mean."

"I know," she said. "I just wanted to make sure you were okay, and say thank you. As horrible as this may sound, their deaths made me feel just a little bit better. Not much, but a little bit. I love you."

"I love you too, Linda. I'll see you soon."

He was dressed by eleven, ready to rumble. He called Gallagher and told him to have the car ready in 15 minutes. Raymond took a last look in the mirror, ran his hands down the front of his clothes for a last-minute smooth, and headed out.

Gallagher was there, along with Archer, in the black Suburban, Shelby behind the wheel. "Take me to the cemetery."

Gallagher knew where he wanted to go, and instructed Shelby to go over the 59th Street Bridge (Raymond refused to call it, or have it called in front of him, the Ed Koch Bridge) to Queens Ridge Cemetery. The gates opened, and Shelby drove slowly through to the reception building. Gallagher went in, registered (under his own name), accepted the carnations that Raymond had specifically ordered—white carnations because they stood for "remembrance," rather than the red roses he had originally wanted, that stood for "passionate love," on smart advice from Gallagher. Shelby drove slowly to the entrance nearest Sheilah Dannis's grave.

Raymond got out, took the flowers from Gallagher, then walked by himself to the still fresh mounds of dirt and flowers and the pristine headstone above Sheilah's grave.

SHEILAH DANNIS
1973–2017
Died in the service of her Country

Raymond laid the flowers across the grave, in front of the head-stone, then knelt down beside the grave. "Sheilah," he said, paused and then continued, "I'm so sorry I wasn't there to protect you." Another pause. "We got the bastards who did this to you. We blew them into a million pieces." Pause. "Sheilah, I . . . I love you so much. You rocked my world in ways I never thought possible. I hope you'll wait for me, wherever you are, and one day we will be together again. I love you so much . . ." With that he leaned over and kissed the grave once, then the headstone, then stood, wiping a tear from his left eye. He turned and went back to where Gallagher, Shelby, and Archer were waiting. He got in the back seat with Gallagher, and Archer got in the front, and Raymond nodded. The Suburban began its slow wind to the exit, headed for the bridge and the city.

Nobody said a word for the entire trip to Police Plaza.

CHAPTER 32

5:30 pm, Tuesday, 12 December

Rick had settled in, looked at the pile of paper-work on his desk, and buzzed in Janey. She came in the office with her pearly white smile and bright blue eyes. "Yes, Commissioner?" There was a familiar note of anxiety in her voice.

"Janey," Raymond said, "have Jerry go through this crap, sign my name wherever it needs to go, and get it out of here."

"I'll take care of it," she said, and started to go.

"Oh," he added. She looked over her shoulder. "And hold all my calls. I don't care if it's Captain America; take a message."

"Who?"

"Never mind; just no calls."

He got up and brewed himself a triple espresso. He couldn't get the smell of those carnations out of his nose. He drank the espresso down in one shot, then went back to his desk. He took out his cell and called Chernova. Her phone rang twice; then the automatic message picked up. He was about to hang up when he heard her breathless voice cut in. That alone gave him a sexual stir. "Rick," she said, clean and crisp."

"How are you, babe?"

"Good, good. Busy, I'm afraid. Lots going on here."

"Can you get away tonight?"

"Oooh . . ."

"The Marcus Hotel at 7:30? We'll order in."

"The Marcus . . . Did you get a pay raise?"

"You could say that," he laughed.

"So, we're ordering in; then what?"

"Then we'll fuck our brains out."

"Well," she said, "I may not be hungry, but I'm starving. See you then. Take your vitamins."

He laughed once to himself as he hung up the phone. He buzzed Gallagher. "Jerry, handle my meetings this afternoon. I'm going to do a little clothes shopping, and I've got to see the attorneys about selling my apartment in Riverdale and Sheilah's brownstone in Brooklyn. Also, let's set something up in the next week or so with the PBA president. I want to give him something for the Widows and Orphans Fund. I also want to start an endowment in Sheilah's name for a scholarship fund for the families of the DA's office.

"Yes sir."

He arrived at the Marcus by seven, and told Shelby and Archer they could get something to eat and then call it a night. The two figured he was in for the evening. They decided to hang out at the bar, have dinner there before heading home.

Raymond got to his suite, slipped into a hot bath, watched the steam rise above his submerged body, scrubbed every inch of his skin with the hotel's sweet and smooth soap, got out, checked his face—no, he needn't shave again, he thought; Mila liked the roughness of his stubble. He splashed a little of the Domenico Vacca scent on his neck. The hotel always stocked it in his suite for him. He liked the arch sweetness of the scent. Manly but not cloying.

He came out with only a towel wrapped around him and went to pour himself a drink. There was a knock at the door. He opened it to see Chernova, dressed from head to toe in black and white—black pants suit, white ruffled shirt, high heels, white gloves, dark glasses with speckled black and white frames. The lenses were so dark he couldn't see her eyes. "Come in, darling," he said. As she stepped in, she smiled and took her glasses off.

"You look and smell divine," she murmured as he handed her a glass of Prosecco.

"So do you. I'm so glad to see you," he said and threw his arms around her, nearly spilling her drink. She giggled softly as she felt his hardness against her, through his towel.

"Shall we eat first or get down to business and break for a late dinner?

"What do you think," he said, as he slipped open the tuck-knot of his towel and let it fall to the ground, exposing his erectness. Her eyes went to it and sparkled, as she leisurely pulled her gloves off her hands. She slowly took her clothes off, until her body was completely naked, except for her stockings and spike heels, her tattoos shining red and blue all over. He embraced her, then lifted her as if carrying her over the threshold into the bedroom, where they proceeded to shake the universe to its Milky Way roots.

It was past eleven when they came up for air. Their bodies stayed stuck together until Raymond pried himself from her. "I hope that snake doesn't bite me," he said softly.

"I think it did."

He leaned up on one hand. "Hungry?"

"Ravenous, darling. You took everything out of me. I need to be replenished!"

"I'll order up."

"Quickly," she said, "so we can eat, then get back to business."

He got up and went to the phone in the living room, ordered two steaks, two small Caesars, a bottle of Pouilly-Fuissé, and two bowls of ice cream he was sure would be drunk, rather than eaten, at two in the morning as post-priandal treat.

For the first time since that attack on Times Square, Raymond experienced some measure of peace. Thank God, he thought, for Mila, as he sat down to wait for the food.

CHAPTER 33

11:45 pm, Tuesday, 12 December

Raymond heard the knock on the door. He peeked into the bedroom and said, "Food is here," then closed the door behind him. "Coming," he said, grabbing the towel from the floor where it had fallen hours earlier and wrapping it around himself.

He opened the door and the room service person rolled the cart in. Raymond immediately sensed something was wrong. He knew all the VIP staff that handled the penthouse and delivered to his suite. As the man wheeled the cart in, an iceberg shot up Raymond's ass. He knew that face. He recognized the eyes from the video, those black, burning, angry eyes! *It was Samadi!* "*You!*" Raymond screamed, with the heat and fury of a fire-breathing dragon. But before he could do anything, Samadi flipped up the cart and threw it in Raymond's direction, food flying everywhere, water, bits of salad, rolls, as if a bomb had exploded.

"*I kill you!*" Samadi said as he pulled his scimitar out from beneath his apron.

He survived, Raymond thought. The bastard got away! He lunged at Samadi, flying through the air, grabbing the hand with the scimitar as he did. But Samadi was strong, very strong, and he caught Raymond by the throat and heaved him against the wall. Raymond was stunned, and shook his head, his eyes clearing just enough to see Samadi, his scimitar held high, coming at him, curses spewing from his mouth. Samadi thrust his scimitar straight at Raymond's neck, but Raymond managed to roll away just in time; and tangling a leg into his attacker, Raymond kicked up with everything he had and sent Samadi falling backward.

Raymond stood up, wobbling, and went for Samadi. He grabbed him by his shirt, through his apron, and lifted him off the ground. "You bastard," he said, holding him with his left hand as he swung a right in a semicircle, landing it squarely on Samadi's face. He heard the sickening crack of bone as Samadi went down. Raymond then kicked him twice in his ribs. There was no way he wasn't going to kill him now. He went down, grabbed Samadi by his hair, and began banging his head on the floor, not wanting to stop until the pieces of Samadi's skull looked like scrabble letters scattered on a bridge table.

He never saw the knife come around and cut into his side. The pain caused Raymond to jerk up, and involuntarily he let go of Samadi. The prick had a razor-sharp blade under his apron. Samadi kicked him off, and Raymond staggered to his feet, blood gushing from his side. He watched, unable to do anything, as Samadi pushed himself up and went for the scimitar. Raymond took a deep breath and dove for it as well. Their bodies collided against each other, as both men, bleeding and weakened, fought like the wounded wild animals they were, to get to the weapon, the loser knowing for sure he wouldn't be allowed to live.

With one last push, Samadi was able to shove Raymond off him. Raymond rolled onto his back, the force of the push having dug the knife deeper into his side. He felt like a hot bag of rice as his blood continued to spurt around the blade in him. Samadi stumbled to the scimitar, grabbed it, and shouted *"Allahu Akbar! God is great!"* as he moved in for the kill. He was going to decapitate the commissioner, just as he had done to Sheilah. Raymond put his left hand up, as if to try to stop what was coming, then braced himself for the worst. He saw Samadi stand above him and raise the sword, and, with a slimy smile on his face, Samadi reached down and grabbed Raymond's hair. "This is personal, you Christian scum."

That's when the shots rang out. Samadi looked up, surprised and quizzical, not understanding what had happened. In the doorway, nude and angry, Mila had held her Glock with her two hands, and after the first shot hit Samadi in his chest, she watched his eyes as he stood shakily, let go of Raymond, and took a step toward her. She fired seven more rounds into his body, until he fell. She walked over to him, kicked him once with her foot. He was twitching and gurgling, with blood spurting out from several wounds, and somehow still alive. Chernova took perfect aim with the red laser from her weapon, watched it for a few seconds as it crazily bounded around Samadi's mouth and teeth, and with one final shot, sent brain matter all over the walls and rugs of the room. "Yes, personal, scumbag," she said between her clenched teeth.

She stood there, her weapon in her hands, as she watched the smoke pour out from what was left of Samadi's head, then realized Raymond was trying to call her but was too weak to shout. She ran over to him, dropped her emptied Glock, and kneeled over him, placing her hands gently on both sides of his face. "How bad?" she said. Then she saw the knife. She grabbed a towel from the bathroom and wrapped it carefully around the still embedded knife to help stop the bleeding, knowing that if she pulled it out, he would bleed to death right there. She knelt over him, kissed his lips, and said softly, "Stay with me, darling. Stay with me." She ran to get her cell phone, returned, knelt beside him as she called Archer in the bar, telling him what happened and that they needed an ambulance. Archer screamed into his radio as he ran to the elevator. *"Code black central, code black—the PC's down. I need a bus forthwith at the Marcus. Code black, the Marcus hotel!"*

Gallagher, Chief Allegra, and what sounded like every cop in the city was heading to the Marcus. Not 90 seconds after Chernova had called, Archer burst through the door, stepping over Samadi to get to Raymond. When he saw the blood-soaked towel and the knife embedded in Raymond, he shouted for Chernova to get another towel. She ran to the bathroom and brought him one. He wrapped it around the blade again and held it in place. Two minutes later, paramedics rushed a gurney through the suite's open door, with Archer waving them in. One pushed Mila away from the body and went to work on Raymond, while another covered his face with an oxygen mask. "We need to get him to the emergency room," the second paramedic said to Archer.

"Bellevue," Archer replied.

"He won't make it that far. New York is the closest. Let's move!" The rest of the emergency team lifted Raymond onto the gurney and rushed him into the hallway, to the service elevator they had brought up to the floor, large enough to get the rolling stretcher in. Gallagher followed, as did Archer, pistol out and pointed up.

"Wait," Mila said, and rushed to the bathroom to grab her robe. She got to the elevator just as it was starting to close. One paramedic already had an IV working. Mila bent over Rick's face and tried to rub it under the mask. "Rick," she said, *"Rick, goddamn you, answer me! Answer me!"*

There was no focus left in his eyes. She turned to one of the paramedics. "Is he going to make it?"

"Out of my way," he said, pushing her away as the elevator hit the lower level. There, an ambulance was waiting. They wheeled the gurney up to the back entrance, collapsing the legs as they pushed it in. Archer jumped in. Mila tried to follow.

"No," the paramedic said.

"Fuck you," she said, and pushed her way in. "Now move this thing out of here. Now!"

She held Rick's hand, afraid of how cold it seemed.

CHAPTER 34

2:35 pm, Wednesday, 13 December

Chernova was sitting in a private room of New York Hospital, surrounded by FBI agents from OPR, the Officer of Professional Responsibility, as well as people from the NYPD's Internal Affairs, The U.S. Attorney's Office was methodically quizzing her about the attack, the stabbing, the shooting. Mayor Brown, Gallagher, Archer, Chief Allegra, and FBI agent Jones were sitting across the hall in a VIP reception room. Raymond had not regained consciousness since the attack. He was breathing with the help of a respirator. He had lost a great deal of blood, and his body had been broken in several places, including most of his ribs and one arm, the one he had used to punch Samadi. The prognosis had been less than 50-50 he would make it, time being of the essence. If he came out of it in the next day or two, he might recover. If he didn't, well, he didn't.

Chernova patiently answered their questions, but all she could think of was Raymond lying in the ER unit. She just wanted him to live. She had known almost from the first minute they met she would fall in love with him. Her first motivation was to help him get over the death of Sheilah. Now, all she wanted was for him to live, for himself, for her.

It was almost three in the afternoon of the third day, when the machine attached to Raymond blipped. A nurse came running out of his room. "Doctor, please, right away!" The resident on the floor ran into the room. Everyone jumped up, and Chernova followed. Try to stop me, she thought to herself as they entered the ER.

The doctor, a young man who looked to Chernova like a college sophomore, was leaning over Raymond. "Can you hear me, sir? Can you hear me? Blink if you can hear me, Commissioner."

Chernova pushed everyone else out of the way as she tried to get a better look at Raymond. Everyone's eyes were glued to Raymond's as they waited.

And waited.

"I'm afraid he's not . . . ," the doctor started to say, when Raymond's eyes fluttered. "Rick," Chernova screamed, and kept pushing her way up, stopped in her tracks by Gallagher, who held her firmly but not roughly.

"Let the doctor work," he said softly.

"Ummnnuuuhhh," Raymond said through his oxygen mask. The doctor lifted it off. "Where . . . where am I?" Raymond said, his raspy voice barely above a whisper.

"You're at New York Hospital," the doctor said.

"Rick," Chernova said, and Gallagher slowly let go of her as she leaned over the bed. "Darling," she said, "I'm here. I'm right here."

Raymond turned his head slowly. "Mila," he said, and smiled as much as he could. "Room service is ready . . ." Then he fell back asleep.

"He's going to make it," the doctor said. "He needs rest. A lot of rest."

"I'm staying here with him," Chernova said.

"Try not to disturb him. He's got a long way to go."

"I'll sit in a chair by his side. I just want to be there when he opens his eyes again."

Jones shook hands with the doctor and thanked him. Brown did as well, then turned to the others: "Jerry, you stay here, and no visits until the doctors says it's all right."

"Yes, sir," Gallagher said. "We've got men on every floor, armed with everything but nuclear bombs. No one will get near him, I guarantee it." He smiled and said to the mayor, "He's a tough guy. A fighter. A good fucking man, Sir."

The mayor put one hand on Gallagher's shoulder. "I know he is, Jerry."

Outside the room, Jones was talking with the resident. "How long do you think he'll have to be here?"

"Depends," the doctor said. "If his brain is working, and it appears to be, and his body heals, it could be as little as three weeks before we can move him out of IC, and then, I don't know, maybe three to four weeks. I think he'll make it. He's through the hardest part. Knife wounds to the torso are deadly and difficult to treat, because the wounds are so insidious. His doctor will be by in a while and give you a better assessment." He paused and then said, "That lady in there—she's as tough as he is."

Gallagher laughed. "Tougher."

CHAPTER 35

10:15 am, Monday, 22 January

It was a day of victory, if not celebration, for Raymond. He was returning to work for the first time since the night at the hotel. He had since learned from Jones how Samadi had gotten into the hotel. He had disguised himself as a food deliverer; then, once inside the hotel kitchen, he hid in cabinets and closets, curled up like a rat, avoiding light, making no noise, waiting for when he knew was the right time to strike. He had with him a computer that he used to hack into the hotel's kitchen. He checked every hour to see who was getting room service, waiting for the time that Raymond returned to the hotel he had read about in the *Herald* as the one he preferred. On the night of his attempt to kill Raymond, he slit the throat of the delivery person, quickly and quietly, dragged him into the meat refrigerator, put on his uniform, and helped to fill the order; he counted on no one paying any attention—nobody in hotel kitchens, he knew, cared about anything except cigarette breaks, free beers from the bar, and the racing sheet; he simply brought the cart up to the room, ready to create new carnage. Jones had described him as bloodthirsty, a political vampire who lived off the blood of his victims.

"You were lucky Mila was there. Of all days for you not to have your gun. And you're lucky Mila is an FBI agent and she had hers with her. She's the reason he's dead and you're alive," Jones had said to him on one of her last visits to the hospital before Raymond was released.

Raymond arrived at work in the Suburban and was helped out of the SUV by Archer, happy to have the commissioner back at work. Raymond was able to get on his feet, now with the help of Gallagher and an aluminum cane. Raymond still had difficulties walking, but that he was walking at all was something of a miracle. Next out of the Surburban was Chernova. Whatever secrets she had between her and Raymond, that was all gone. She had been hailed as a hero for saving his life and killing Samadi. Her anonymity was gone, but she didn't care. She didn't care about anything, as long as Raymond was alive.

The press was out in force. Rick's unsteady walk to his private elevator in the garage at Police Plaza, holding on to Gallagher, would be seen in every living room in the country that evening, and around the world, thanks to the press pool camera arranged by Deputy Commissioner Thomas. As Raymond walked, in pain and limping, he kept his stoic manner and ignored the camera.

In his absence, Raymond's first deputy, Joe Nagle, had assumed the commissioner's duties. Now, a ceremony was planned, with the mayor to officially greet Rick on his return to full duty (and, of course, the press played it up as a political show since the primaries were only months away), but Raymond knew better. Mayor Brown had been to the hospital three or four times a week, most often not even seen by the press.

The ceremony was brief, the press got it on the record, and then Gallagher ushered everybody out of the office, except Jones and Chernova. Archer stood outside the door, and gave Janey a quick glance. Janey noticed Archer and smiled at him, before reaching for the phone. It was ringing off the hook.

Raymond sank down in his chair and let out a deep breath. "I never thought I'd see the inside of this place again."

"We're glad to have you back," Jones said.

"Where've you been? I didn't see you all last week."

"Yes I know; something came up, something pretty important."

"Not about this, right?" Raymond said. "Samadi's dead, isn't he?"

"Yes, he's dead," Jones said. "But it's not the end, we're afraid."

Raymond sat up. "What do you mean?"

"Mila, do you want to fill him in?"

Chernova sat on one side of the desk. "Rick, last week I got a call to come in. The Bureau had gone through most of the phone lines and thought it had everything, when a new message was discovered, from the day of the Wall Street and school attack. No one was able to crack the code. The tech guys worked on it every day for a week. That's where I was when I was gone every day. They finally figured it out."

"The bottom line?" Raymond said.

"We always thought that Samadi was the number one guy, the cell leader."

Raymond said nothing, as his eyes narrowed.

Jones picked up the story. "But it looks like he was working for another guy that's somewhere in Qatar. His name is Muhammad Hamza, code name 'The Ghost.' No one at the Bureau or at CIA had ever heard of him before. We have nothing on him, no face, no history, nothing. Apparently he used their no-call code to leave one final message for Samadi. He wanted his group of maniacs to bring down the Empire State Building next and, for some nutty reason, the statue of George M. Cohan in Duffy Square, in the heart of Broadway. Anyway, there was nothing else after their attacks failed.

No more messages. We know he's out there, and he's the one who's been calling all the shots; apparently, Samadi was answering to this guy Hamza."

"So, let's get this guy," Raymond said.

"Not so easy. As I said, we have no idea who he is, what he looks like, nothing," Jones said.

"Don't tell me we can't find him. Why can't we go to Qatar. I'll go myself."

"Commissioner, you can barely walk; you're not going anywhere," Gallagher said.

"This Hamza may be known as The Ghost, but he's flesh and blood and can be caught. He's got to be stopped, or Samadi will be replaced and the attacks will continue."

"I agree," Jones said. "It looks like the White House is going to authorize DOJ, the CIA, and the Department of Defense to put together an elite special operations team to identify him, locate him, and capture or kill him."

"I'll do it myself," Raymond said, as the group looked at him as if he were delusional.

"Really, Rick," Jones said. "The most celebrated New York City police commissioner in the country's history is going to sneak into Qatar on his white horse and snatch Hamza or kill him? You need your fucking head examined. How are you going to get in? How are you going to get a visa? Where are you going to tell the press you're going and for how long? Use your fucking head, because right now you sound like a fucking nut."

"Okay." Raymond said. "Maybe you're right, but I want in on this."

"I knew you would. So here's the deal. You'll take a six-month leave from the NYPD, be appointed as special envoy to the Emirates by the president, and be assigned to the U.S. Embassy in Qatar. You'll oversee this special operations group and make sure Hamza is brought to justice. That's the only way you're going to be involved, and let's face it, that's the only way we're going to get him. Are you in, or are you out?"

"I'll crawl if I have to. Hamza's ass is mine. I'm in!"

The room became silent. Jones crossed her arms, stared at Rick, and said nothing.

"And I'm going with him," Chernova said, breaking the silence.

"Me too," said Gallagher.

He looked around the room. Nobody said a word. Mila went over and stood behind Raymond's chair. He reached up and took her hand and squeezed it. She leaned over and kissed the top of his head.

"You leave on Monday," Jones said.

Raymond sat there staring at the others, waiting to see if anyone had anything else to say. Then he broke the silence.

"Here we go again."